CHRIS POWER

The Calling

A Philosophical Novel

The Calling

ISBN (Print): 978-1-09830-317-4
ISBN (eBook): 978-1-09830-318-1

For my father

Acknowledgements

I want to thank my wife Diane for her inexhaustible patience and encouragement as I worked — and often failed to work— to achieve my goal. Hers is an example I will follow as I try to support others.

Table of Contents

Chapter 1

Metamorphosis

Somehow I had beaten the Friday traffic leaving Manhattan, sailing through the Lincoln Tunnel at 2:00 in the afternoon. I emerged on the Jersey side to find a scorching autumn sun, already in descent. I must have stared for too long—when I turned away its afterimage left a dark hole in my vision. I turned my eyes back to the road. I was thrilled to be ahead of the wave, that great tide of humanity called the New York City rush hour. I had dodged a phenomenon as certain as death and taxes. A very good start to the weekend.

But something was not right. Every glance at the dashboard clock reminded me how little I had accomplished that day. I couldn't escape the feeling of continuously falling behind. With that thought, a black wave of anxiety rose like bile in my gut, seized my chest and throat in its cold grip. I exhaled forcefully, trying to relax my grip on the wheel.

The blighted landscape of the New Jersey Turnpike—its gray, repetitious misery, its miles of lines, signs, barriers, and rails—forced my attention inward. Thoughts and images rose up one by one, like bubbles from a dark well. One bubble burst on the surface and released a message: *"the remains of the day"*. A distinct sinking feeling followed in its wake.

It was already autumn; school was back in session, the leaves were falling, the nights were getting cold. Another year had come and gone—but what did I have to show for it? What had happened to my personal goals? What had happened to the "better self" I once imagined so clearly? Had it been permanently sidelined by daily demands and worries?

As I fixed my eyes on the traffic ahead, another bubble rose up and released the message: *"rue the day..."*. What did that mean? Another bubble immediately followed: *"Rue Morgue."* Poe's murder-mystery? What could it mean? *Rue*—regret, or road? I tried to focus on the road.

These dark epiphanies, which over the past few months had come more and more frequently, no longer alarmed me. I found my mind wandering along these morbid paths continously now, particularly when I was alone. Was it depression? Maybe—but I had never really suffered depression. My mind and mood had always been predictable and steady. Apparently, that sound mind was a thing of the past.

I lowered the car window a few inches to clear my head. But soon, in the white noise of the wind, I could hear a faint woodwind melody, in a minor key. I struggled to place it, until I heard a mournful voice sing: *Buss und Reu, Buss und Reu, knirscht das Sündernherz entzwei*. Bach's Saint Matthew Passion…I hadn't heard it for a long time, but it came back clearly now, as if I were hearing it on the radio. *Buss und Reu*—regret and rue. Why this song, why now?

As I turned on to the New York State Thruway mountains appeared, with orange, yellow, and russet leaves glowing in the sunshine. But soon clouds swept over the mountain and the scene changed into one of barren gray winter hills. This change was accompanied by somber feelings of impermanence and uncertainty. A mere change of wind had brought these vulnerable feelings. What was happening to me? Where was my infallible inner optimist?

A few months ago, something strange had happened to me. I woke up one bright June morning to a world emptied of meaning. Outwardly, the world looked more or less the same, except for one oddity: everything had been reduced to the same value. Nothing looked more important than anything else. My values had been flattened overnight. So it was impossible to determine what I should do next.

I had stared at the bedroom ceiling, searching for a reason to get up. None was forthcoming. Usually I'd wait for some motive, like coffee, to propel my feet to the floor. But that day—nothing. I was an inert block of matter. After much labored reasoning I forced myself, still lacking any justification, to put my feet on the floor and stand. Looking out my window I saw people hurrying about, like typical New Yorkers. But it was no longer clear to me why they should be rushing, or where they might be going. Suddenly, their intentions were alien to me. I saw my children leave for school, with resounding slams of the front door; I saw my wife getting ready for work. But I could not quite grasp why. The importance of these things now escaped me. Meaning had bled out of these things—out of the world— overnight. Without the guidance of these certainties, I had no idea what to do next.

Maybe the world and the things in it *had* no built-in meaning or value. Maybe it had been an illusion all along, an illusion that made it possible to live. Had meaning and value drained from my psyche, like a cracked pot, overnight?

I forced myself mechanically through the morning rituals, got my body out of the door and off to work. I got through the first day by overcompensating, by pretending to be interested in everything. I struggled to find my bearings, but eventually found a routine I could sustain. My strategy would be to minimally satisfy the demands of work and life as I tried to figure out what was going on.

Suddenly I no longer found satisfaction in comforting routines, like morning coffee, reading the newspaper, and walking my dog Juno. Even long-standing pleasures, like fiction and photography, had lost their appeal. Nothing seemed worth reading, nothing seemed worth photographing. I even lost interest in having a drink at the end of the day: even my vices were no longer compelling. I knew something was seriously wrong.

Misfortune has finally tracked me down, I thought. But how could I be surprised? I had been lucky for so long. I had a happy family, a good job, a home in the city, a house in the country, freedom to come and go as I pleased. I had good friends, old and new. Though I wasn't rich, I considered myself more fortunate than pretty much anyone. But why should this good fortune continue? Deep down, I never really expected it to last forever.

But even when we brace for misfortune, it never comes in the expected way. Maybe we can prepare for financial loss, or sickness, or even the loss of someone we love. But how does one prepare to lose interest in life? I had taken this interest totally for granted. Life, it seems, had played a cruel trick on me. Its riches, and my purpose in it, were whisked away before my eyes. And I sensed that no pill, no therapy, no vacation could restore it.

New initiatives at work demanded my attention, so I had no choice but to put my head down and soldier on. I would have to show up every morning and maintain the appearance of a serious, successful person, until I figured out what to do. I would have to operate *incognito.*

Chapter 2

Goal Setting

Suddenly I was aware that I was driving, and found myself exiting the Thruway. My hands turned the wheel toward the tollgate; they knew exactly what to do. I did not so much steer the car as watch it *being* steered as it cut over to the *EZ Pass Only* lane. Coming out of the tollbooth, my body handled these interactions with a smooth precision my conscious mind could never match. It drove, via on-ramps and off-ramps, with little help from the so-called "higher" functions. I watched as body and car, a single mechanism, turned onto Route 28 West.

Last month, my friend Rich called to tell me he was hosting a seminar for a renowned business coach at his summer house. The seminar would be a private coaching session for Rich, his investors, board members, and business associates. He wanted me to attend. The famous coach—infamous to his critics—had developed a new seminar called "Reach for Greatness." In it, he challenged his students to attempt to achieve their highest goal—or to "fail greatly" trying. The coach was known for his brilliance, his melodrama, and his temper. He was a prima donna—but one who supposedly provoked results. His followers included notable CEOs and business gurus—people who could afford his outrageous fees.

About a week later Rich asked me to meet him for drinks at his swanky uptown club, the Core Club. Subdued, tasteful, modern art everywhere. I found him at his favorite table near the end of the bar, answering emails. Rich looked up, raised his eyebrows in mock surprise, and nodded at the two drinks in front of him.

"I knew you would need this," he said with a smile.

I recognized Rich's tactics. Steep your targets in luxury, beauty, and alcohol, and they are far more pliant. Pretty good strategy, but I was having none of it.

I sank into the club chair opposite him, took a sip of my drink —a Manhattan straight up—and prepared for the coming charm offensive.

As it happened, Rich was not in a charming mood. He went right at me.

"Don't even think about saying 'no'. You are adrift, my friend, and this is an intervention. Tell me you're coming, man, and no waffling."

I took a deep draught of my drink, which, being straight alcohol, had the needed bracing effect. I was in a tough spot. Rich was right, but I had to reject his offer. I could barely find the motivation to show up for work, so far was I from attempting something "great".

I objected. "Dude, I simply do not belong at that table. I'm neither a mover nor a shaker. It will just make me feel small."

"Nonsense, you're coming!" Rich declared, confident his case was closed. He set down his drink—an Old-Fashioned in an heavy crystal glass—firmly and precisely to underline his point. "Your argument is absurd: you are unable to make a decision, and therefore someone must make it for you. I am that someone, coming through for you again."

I desperately needed change—but also feared what it might bring. My future had gone dark. Though I had no idea what to do, I resisted.

"Okay—maybe you're right. But I don't have three thousand dollars to plunk down on a whim. The fact that I cannot afford this seminar is sufficient proof that I don't belong there."

Rich looked offended. "Don't get me wrong, man. It's on me, you're my guest." It was a sunken cost, he insisted. His company had already paid for it. One of his business partners had to drop out because of a last-minute conflict.

My heart sank. Now it was impossible to refuse. It was a generous offer. But more than that, I couldn't ignore Rich's intent. He was a very good friend, and he was looking out for me.

That was three weeks ago, to the day.

As I drove west, with the sun sinking behind the hills, a calendar alarm sounded on my cell phone. I glanced quickly at the screen:

REACH FOR GREATNESS

Anxiety rose again, like bile in the back of my throat. I exhaled forcibly to push it back down. What did it even mean, "reach for greatness"? I really did not want to go to this thing. I have always had a dim view of motivational seminars. Perhaps my early bad experience formed this view. In the late seventies, all my best friends did EST (Erhard Seminar Training) but I refused. Despite the pleas and passionate testimonials from the most important people in my life, I rejected it outright. At EST "coffees" (to which my friends recruited me), I stood with arms folded, parrying skeptically with true believers who tried to convince me how unhappy I was. They were absolutely sure that there was a hole in my life that needed filling. They presumed to know me, which I found offensive.

For Rich's sake though, I would try to keep an open mind. I knew that this seminar required choosing a great goal—an achievement we would measure ourselves by, and be remembered by. But I couldn't stop my inner skeptic's immediate response: *Why demand any more of ourselves than a decent life requires? Why torment ourselves with perpetual dissatisfaction? Can't we, at some point, declare the striving over? Can't we just climb Maslow's pyramid, find satisfaction in what we have, and call it a day?*

So much for keeping an open mind.

Joseph Campbell once called Maslow's hierarchy of values "the values for which people live when they have nothing to live for." Nothing, he said, had seized them, nothing had caught them, nothing had driven them spiritually mad and made them worth talking to.[1] For Campbell, self-actualization merely checked off all the boxes of a healthy ego—of individual, social, and conventional adequacy. His view: Is that all there is? For each person also has an inner trajectory, a spiritual path, that carries them along—they know not where. Unconsciously we follow this path, which fate has drawn for us. There may be some neurosis in the overachiever. But beneath their overt ambitions and compulsive energy is an innate desire for inner growth. This desire is at bottom not neurosis, but an unconscious yearning for spiritual transformation. Or as Campbell would have it, for a journey of transformation.

Suddenly, I was blinded by a brilliant light. A pickup truck was coming toward me in the opposite lane, its high beams at eye level. I drove past it and turned left on a gravel road. A few uncertain miles later I turned again onto a narrow dirt road, with dense woods pressing right up to the edge. Through the woods I saw lights, then a clearing, then cars, and finally a big white house set against a starry sky. *Here we go,* I thought. There was no turning back now.

Chapter 3

The Coach

I drove past the row of cars parked on the lawn—Mercedes, Audi, BMW, Lexus. It looked like a foreign car dealership. I parked my Honda minivan at the end of the row.

Rich had organized a dinner for guests arriving the night before, including the coach. Most of them were from Rich's private equity firm, or were investors in it. On the big wraparound porch, and inside the front room of the house, young financial guys, unreasonably fit and groomed, wearing expensive shirts and shoes, talked in groups.

I found Rich in the living room talking to two guys, Anastas and James, who were partners in his firm. They were talking about an upcoming CrossFit competition. Anastas, a tall, friendly Hollander with a wispy blond beard, made me feel welcome. He seemed to know everyone—and, in fact, it turns out he was a neighbor of mine. This made me feel like a peer, on equal footing. He lived only a few blocks from my apartment in the Village. But when I realized which house was his—a sleek modern townhouse which he had designed himself—my heart sank. *Incalculably expensive,* I thought. *Not on equal footing.*

This is what happens in Manhattan. You feel pretty good about yourself, you feel reasonably accomplished, and, by global standards, you are in fact very fortunate. But then you meet someone whose wealth or degree of accomplishment dwarfs your own. Your achievements seem as nothing. You immediately have doubts, and wonder what you have done with your life. What seemed great just a moment ago now seems small, and you must put on blinders to rebuild your sense of self-worth.

The only consolation to these demoralizing comparisons is that it happens to everyone, including the super-rich. A fund manager earning several million dollars a year can come away from a lunch with another fund manager feeling like a pauper. I can't say I sympathize with him much.

However, an excellent and free-flowing cabernet helped promote good feeling all around. Talk gradually rose to a rowdy din as we waited for the coach to arrive. At nine o'clock, hunger finally took over. Rich commandeered a massive grill on the porch, and cooked rib eye steaks, eggplants, and green beans. In short order, dinner was on the table—and then, shortly thereafter, it was gone.

Around 10:30 the doorbell rang—the coach. As he stepped through the doorway, his demeanor contrasted sharply with our shouting, music, and litter of wine bottles. He entered with a grave bow, and no hint of emotion. He was tall and thin, with an aristocratic forehead, a long face, and a discontented look. He was dressed in gray and black—in bespoke clothes that fit his trim body perfectly—including a black, woolen cape, which he wore convincingly. He recalled the older Herbert von Karajan. His flowing gray hair, imperious manner, and severe "European" comportment was a rebuke to our rowdy American enthusiasm. His presence immediately sucked the life out of the room. After a curt greeting to the group, he asked to be shown to his room.

As Rich led the coach upstairs, the rest of us stole glances at each other, with the collective thought: what a bummer. This guy was all business. He did not enjoy our bonhomie. He had probably had a bad flight, and a long drive from the airport. Or maybe he was just a big drag. His harsh demeanor set us all back on our heels. Clearly, we had gotten started on the wrong foot. We said our good nights and went to our rooms, wondering what this encounter might imply for tomorrow's seminar.

As usual, I couldn't sleep. So I Googled the coach, Miloš Janáček, and learned the following.

Janáček was born Miloš Nagy in Budapest in 1952 to a Hungarian father and Czech mother. Given the year of his birth, his earliest memories may well have been the sirens, panic, and gunfire that accompanied the Soviet tanks rolling into that city in '56. His father rashly joined a militia and was shot dead in the first week of the invasion. In '57 his mother took him to Prague, to live with her brother's family. Miloš hated his last name—Nagy, the name of Hungary's great traitor—so he eventually took his mother's (and uncle's) name, Janáček.

Janáček came of age during the Prague Spring, turning sixteen in '68—only to witness the Soviets invade his home again, this time to crush the Czech liberation movement. By then he was a hippie and street activist. He was arrested, like so many other Prague Spring agitators, for subversion. While in Soviet custody, he twice attempted suicide. But after being released from prison, he found redemption in the form of a Czech "cultural exchange program" with Moscow State University, which offered degree programs to Czech students. Janáček attended the lectures of the great Hungarian psychologist László Garai. He displayed a gift for psychology, and with Garai's urging, embarked on a PhD program under Alexsei Leontiev, the developmental psychologist who had founded the MSU Department of Psychology only a year before.

Leontiev was one of the founders of Activity Theory, a school of psychology that swept Russian academia in the '70s and Europe in the '80s. Janáček became his youngest and most brilliant student, earning a PhD in psychology at the age of twenty-four. He stayed on as adjunct faculty, doing research and teaching, until 1979, when Leontiev died of a heart attack.

Here the history of Janáček went dark for more than twenty years. His last known contact with his family was during a brief trip to Prague in the summer of 1979. This gap, I knew, corresponded to similar gaps in the careers of many Russian and Eastern European psychologists, who disappeared behind the Iron Curtain around this time. Many were "commissioned" by the military to conduct mind control experiments, based on an emerging pseudoscience called *Psychotronics*. Psychotronics was basically a state-sponsored attempt to read and control the minds of the public on a mass scale, for military and political purposes. Janáček's reputation for scientific rigor, his brilliance in devising psychological experiments, his lack of family contacts and connections in Russia, and the recent loss of his mentor—all of this made him a prime candidate for recruitment into the top-secret program. It was conducted in the remotest parts of the former USSR, and precluded all contact with family or colleagues in the West.

This all seemed pretty far-fetched, until I learned that the CIA had their own mind control program during the Cold War, with the far sexier name MKUltra. Anyway, little more is known about Janáček or his whereabouts until he resurfaced in 2010 as a lecturer in psychology at Bard College. During his two years there he wrote a book, *Reach for Greatness*. From this book he developed a seminar with the same name. In the five years since, he had built a devoted—even fanatical—following. He advocated ruthless self-critique and naked candor. He was skeptical of money and power. Despite these idiosyncrasies, his reputation grew, and his seminars became coveted as the ultimate "thinking CEO's" credential. His fees grew accordingly.

His seminars had earned their controversy. For example, though most attendees were business people, business goals were specifically excluded from his seminar. Revenue, profitability, market share—as far as Janáček was concerned, this was all twaddle. In his view, business goals, driven by profit, very rarely have intrinsic value. They are limited by their self-interest and pragmatism. For Janáček, there was only one question: how do we, as individuals, overcome our limitations to achieve our next stage of inner growth? This concern is much more fundamental than business goals. Thus his seminar focused exclusively on personal goals.

Another source of controversy: Janáček himself judged the worthiness of each participant's goal. If he thought that a goal did not advance the personal growth of the participant, he would instruct them to choose another goal—or assign one to them. In fact, this was a contractual condition of the seminar. To a group of New Yorkers paying thousands of dollars, probably expecting to be catered to, this had to be unpalatable. On the other hand, the goals that Janáček assigned had the reputation of being spot-on perfect for each person. It became a badge of honor to be assigned a goal by Miloš Janáček.

Given what I had learned about his personal history—from his early resistance to totalitarianism, to his participation in KGB-sponsored mind control experiments—Janáček frankly made me nervous. Who was this guy? Who would allow a stranger to choose their highest personal goal?

Chapter 4

The Seminar

Coming downstairs the next morning, I found Janáček sitting ramrod straight at the kitchen table, as though he were waiting to be served. "Good morning", I said, "would you like some coffee?"

I received a polite reply –"Yes, thank you."

I knew my way around the house, so I made coffee and attempted small talk, with no success. Soon we were joined by Rich and some others. Few of us had finished breakfast when Janáček rose silently from the table and walked to the living room. We followed sheepishly along. At precisely nine o'clock, he began the seminar.

"Gentlemen." He nodded to each of us as we settled in chairs and sofas around the big room. "I regret missing dinner last night. My flight was delayed. But I trust we are now rested and ready for the day. We have so much to do, so let's dive right in.

"As a psychologist and clinical researcher, my professional interest is in motivation. I have always been fascinated by what motivates people. Motive is the engine of the world's greatest novels. In *Crime and Punishment* why does Raskolnikov kill the helpless—though vile—old pawnbroker? There is little chance you will put the book down before you find out. In *Anna Karenina* why does the heroine abandon a perfect family and social respectability to pursue the womanizer Count Vronsky? You are compelled to discover what drives her. Motive is at the heart of character. It is a decisive criterion for detectives and prosecutors in establishing guilt. In my last book, *Reach for Greatness*—I have a copy here for each of you—I devoted an entire chapter[1] to character and motive, if you want to explore this question further.

"One of the most powerful motivators is fear of death. Extraordinary acts of bravery and tremendous physical feats have been reported in life-or-death situations—for example, in war, or a general disaster, or getting lost in the wilderness, etcetera. The fear of imminent death causes us to abandon every scruple, giving us access to hidden human powers. In such dire circumstances, death motivates us negatively, or defensively.

"But death also motivates us another way, which we could call *positive*. Awareness of the inevitability of death and its incessant march—always getting closer, no matter how distracted we are by a sense of comfort and security—can provide positive motivation by focusing our attention on the unknown remainder of our lives. Awareness of death implicitly demands a plan: 'What must I do with the rest of my life?'

"To paraphrase Samuel Johnson, nothing clarifies the mind like the hangman's noose. The two years I spent in Soviet detention taught me this much. Not long after the Soviets invaded Prague in August of sixty-eight, I was rounded up and arrested, along with many other street agitators and 'subversives'. I happened to be with a group of students who were throwing Molotov cocktails at tanks. My first cellmate was tortured and beaten then finally strangled to death, with a wet towel, before my eyes. I had no reason to believe my fate would be different. When you are counting the days or hours you have to live, every moment is precious and demands total concentration.

"Death can reveal our most important values. Heidegger's concept of 'being toward death'—*Sein-zum-Tode*—proposes that clarity about one's own death is essential to individual 'authenticity'. In his inimitable poetry, Heidegger calls death 'one's ownmost potentiality for being'. A proper understanding of death is essential—not in the end, but now and at every moment—to the discovery of one's authentic self.

"Can we somehow access the life-changing power of death, without our lives being directly threatened? How can we capture its motivating power to drive us to our highest potential? In the face of death, what great things might we achieve?

"The answer to this question is not the popular notion of a 'bucket list', a touristic interpretation of preparing for death. For that notion is about broadening one's experience. We cannot meet death on its terms while we are diverted from one experience to another. Varied experience helps us forget death. To wrestle with death, to meet it on its own terms and leverage its power, requires a different sort of undertaking. It requires a *single* goal that strains our capacity to the utmost, leaving nothing in reserve. Not through varied outer experiences but by one Great Goal alone do we encounter death and the opportunity to master it. And that is the primary purpose of this seminar, to help you find your one Great Goal.

"By 'great' I means three things. First, the goal must be a true challenge for the goal setter, who will need to draw on their deepest inner reserves to achieve it. In other words there must be a substantial risk of failure. For this reason, the Great

Goal must be an individual achievement. Its value comes from exhausting one's own reserves, not others'. Second, the goal must feel inwardly, subjectively *necessary*. It must have unquestioned value to you. It cannot be a means to an end; it must be an end in itself. Finally, this goal will serve as a legacy, as something we wish to be remembered by.

"I have corresponded with some of you extensively, as you attempted to determine on your own what the goal is, or should be. I am frankly concerned that I have not heard from the rest of you, because choosing the Great Goal can be quite tricky. It is rarely easy or obvious what this might be. It must strain the limits of your ability because it is in fact an attempt to reach beyond yourself. You must prioritize this goal above all others, and may need to dedicate a great deal of time and energy to achieve it. For this reason you must not commit to a goal that does not feel *necessary*.

"From our correspondence it appears that many of you are on the right track; others may need to find another goal. In any case, I've set aside some time for one-on-one meetings with each of you. Some will have doubts, quite naturally. Everyone varies subtly in these things. But at the end of the day, as you Americans are fond of saying, you will have chosen a life-defining goal, and declared it before the rest of the group.

"As you know from the materials you received from my colleague Kamila, we are not focusing on business goals today. Business goals, for the purposes of this seminar, are compromised by their pragmatic bent. Business goals are means to ends. Though they may be very rewarding, it is rare that they have truly intrinsic value. I know that the line separating an entrepreneur from his business is not fixed and clear, and in some cases my proscription here may be unfair. But it is very rare that one's business goals are identical with one's deepest personal values and goals. More often, they are a means to achieve these goals. Bill Gates had an audacious business goal: global dominance of the PC software market. A Windows computer for every person in the world. That vision catapulted Microsoft to a company of tremendous extrinsic value. This enabled Gates to attempt the far more audacious—and intrinsically valuable—personal goal of saving millions of lives by the eradication of malaria. The latter goal is his greatest contribution, his true legacy to the world, worthy in and of itself, and the achievement that will represent him best in remembrance."

There was a uneasy silence in the room. Behind me, someone coughed nervously. There was a good chance that, like me, the other guys here were proud of their business achievements, and did not like having it radically discounted. Competition, winning, profit and reward: these things are baked into business owners, and by disavowing these motives, the coach had moved us—deliberately I am sure—onto uncertain ground.

Janáček pressed on.

"In my first book, *The Phenomenon of Choice,* I explored the conflict of goal setting with our natural roles. One of the great paradoxes of modernity, as it came to accept the basic precepts of science (such as material causation), is that even highly educated people believe that our actions are caused by our intentions and motives. We perversely insist in this belief in free will though we know the truth is otherwise. We need motives to explain, after the fact, why we did what we did. Indeed only by this illusion of our individual agency are conscious, deliberate actions possible.

"The conviction that our intentions and actions are freely chosen stems from what Schopenhauer regarded as an illusion based on *natural bias.*[2] Like everyone here, I passionately want to believe in my individual freedom—but I'm afraid all evidence points in the opposite direction. When we examine our intentions and actions closely, we can always find their cause or ground in an external *force* (what the environment compels us to do); in physical *forms* (what an object does or how a creature acts, according to how it is formed or made); in social *conformity* (what social forces compel us to do); or in mental *reflection* (what motives or inner causes impel us to do). The illusion of freedom is certainly preferable to the truth—namely, that our choices and actions are exhaustively determined by a necessary series of material causes. This is the crux of a distinctly modern dilemma: knowing we are not free, how should we act? What should we do next? On the authority of physical science we know that our actions are not (objectively) free; and yet we (subjectively) *must* be free in order to find meaning in our actions. Maintaining this sense of freedom, illusory or otherwise, is necessary for human life.

"To summarize, there is no basis for individual freedom in the objective world. If it exists at all, it will be found in inner, intentional life. But most, if not all, of inner life is also determined by objective causes. So our first task is to dispel the illusions of freedom that inner life present to us. In *The Phenomenon of Choice,* I attempted this. I tried to show how even our most intimate thoughts and intentions are not spontaneously generated, but rather given by nature, culture and circumstances. My method there was a process of elimination, discounting the myriad causes affecting intentional human behavior—physical, biological, social— to determine if anything like freedom of the will remains. This is why I provided a chapter from that book—which Kamila sent you in an email attachment—as assigned reading.[3]

"After following that process of elimination rigorously to the very end, there appears to remain a certain kind of intentional act that does not labor under the illusion of freedom. This act grasps the goal as physically determined, yet embraces that determinism as one's own. The goal setter paradoxically chooses necessity. Once a person grasps the full depth of determinism, they might recoil in horror and withdraw back into the illusion of freedom. But alternatively, they might embrace this determinism, and pursue what, in individual terms, is called destiny. Destiny is the full identification of conscious choice with necessity. Destiny is external necessity felt as internal or subjective necessity. In the choice of one's destiny may lie the possibility of freedom.

"Most goals focus on changing one's outward circumstances or environment. For example we have plans to improve our home, our body, our job, our material circumstances. But we also pursue goals to change our *inner* circumstances. For example, unhappiness, self-doubt, self-discipline, and negative emotions are inner circumstances we wish to change. When we do attempt this change, it is in conformity to the idea of a higher, better self. The pursuit of inner change has an ancient name: character development. Character development is the process of affecting lasting inner change. But this process is slow and difficult.

"Great athletes know that mastering the forms of their sport is just the beginning. For mastery of the mind, of emotions, fear and doubt—that is the 'inner game' essential to greatness. Hastening inner change is the subject of my book *Reach for Greatness,* and the goal of this seminar.

"What great accomplishment will define you? What great goal is in YOU?" His eyes fixed on each person in the room, one by one, with a mesmerizing intensity. He addressed the group, but his words seemed directed at me alone. Anxiety rose again, like bile in my throat. What was my Great Goal? My heart sank. I had no idea.

The coach concluded his remarks:

"Our next group session will begin an hour from now. During this interval, we will compose letters to be read by our loved ones after our death. The purpose of this is to help clarify what you absolutely *must* achieve before you die. In the meantime I'll call on each of you for quick one-on-one meetings to review your proposed Great Goal. A snack has been prepared for you, but please do not waste time fraternizing over coffee."

I grabbed a bagel and some coffee and headed out to the porch, to give some thought to my goal. I had a long-standing goal to run the New York City Marathon, so I thought: perfect—this was my opportunity to take on that goal. I thought this was a fine challenge, a true test of discipline and grit. I was a runner, but I'd never run more than five or six miles.

Who would question the greatness of the New York City Marathon, which is challenging by any measure? The coach had even mentioned it specifically. Training for the race would provide the added benefit of distracting me from my existential funk. I could focus on this one thing, and in the end, I would have the satisfaction of having achieved something meaningful. And that would be good enough for me.

When finally he called me to meet, his first question brushed aside these justifications.

"Why have you chosen this goal?" the coach demanded.

I answered, "Several friends of mine have run the Marathon and told me what a fulfilling experience it was."

He looked doubtful. "There is nothing wrong with this goal, per se. In fact, one of your colleagues has chosen this same goal, and it is entirely appropriate for him, for various reasons. But for you, I am dubious. I want you to give this more thought. You will have a chance to change your mind, if you decide to do so, later today."

His intuition was uncanny and gave me serious doubts. In fact, I had not come up with this goal for the seminar. I had first thought of running the Marathon a few years ago. I just re-appropriated this goal to the seminar, and the Coach had somehow intuited this. Was it outwardly or inwardly driven? Was it truly *necessary* for me? In Milos Janáček's judgment, no. He could not see it.

"Mr. Donelan, I have the impression that you have not understood the assigned reading. Do you have any questions about it?"

Obviously he could see right through me. It would have been useless to lie.

"I have to tell you, I have not read it."

His eyes widened and he drew a long breath as he struggled to conceal his irritation. He looked down his long nose as if deeply offended.

"How can this be? There is no room in my seminar for the cavalier. This endeavor is deadly serious. You will not find in your remaining years—or days, for all you know—a subject more serious. Yet you arrive totally unprepared."

"Mr. Janáček," I replied, my voice quavering, "please forgive me—but there is no fault. Rich invited me just two weeks ago. I did not receive any emails from Kamila. Normally I'm a diligent student. What can I do?"

"Well that is unfortunate, indeed," Janáček replied, softening his tone. "But it explains why you have proposed this goal. As I said, there is nothing wrong with the goal, per se. It may be something you desire, for various reasons. But is not inwardly *necessary* for you.

"Anyway, you are at a distinct disadvantage. Because even if you quickly grasp the concepts on the assigned pages—which is by no means certain—it takes some time for the true significance of the Great Goal to sink in. Your only hope is to take this—" he handed me a Xerox copy of a chapter from his first book[4]— "and read what you can during our next break. But first, you must finish composing your letter to your survivors. Everyone will have a second one-on-one session with me later this afternoon. To give you a little more time, I'll call on you last."

Chapter 5

The Basement

After lunch we read aloud the letters we had written to our loved ones. Though most of the guys seemed competitive and hard-edged, they each embraced the exercise earnestly. Tender thoughts and tears flowed freely. As each read their letters, I could begin to see Janáček's intent: to move past the abstract notion of death, and explore its emotional content.

I was older than the other guys in the room, part of a generation of men raised to avoid expressing weakness or pain. Growing up in a conservative Catholic household with seven siblings, no attention was paid to exploring emotions, or, in the case of the boys, even acknowledging them. We did not have "quality time" with our parents; we had almost *no* time. My parents raised us as they had been raised. The regular order was stoicism punctuated by threats. My folks were, no doubt, more tender and enlightened than their parents, but still very old-school about discipline. Dad reinforced the expectation that "boys don't cry." I knew these views had been invalidated, but old attitudes die hard.

Thus I admired these younger men who expressed their feelings so readily, without being able to do it myself. I dreaded reading aloud my letter to my daughters. I wanted to commit to the exercise as deeply as the others, but I feared I would fall short. Finally, I was up.

Clearing my throat, I felt all eyes upon me.

" 'Sophia and Jane, if you are reading this, I am already gone. I've withdrawn into that final mystery, death. As I write this I feel my love for you both, and for your mom, in all its power and beauty. To me, you three are life itself. Mom and I were so fortunate to bring you both into the world—healthy, happy, beautiful girls—to help you with your first steps, to guide you to maturity, and marvel as you became women. Of all the wonders of my life, the feelings I experienced with you and through you, as a father, were perhaps the greatest of all.

" 'I could never have done it alone. As hard as I tried (and believe me, I struggled), I could not understand all the things you were going through, especially as teenagers. I did not have the emotional skills. I needed your mom's help. She is gifted, you see. She has great emotional power, an understanding based on love and compassion that dwarfs my analytical view of things. She helped me understand each of you in your own way. She spoke both your language and mine. She translated what you felt—what, as a very different creature, I had little chance of understanding.

" 'Know that the love I felt for each of you was no less than Mom's. I tried my best, but I couldn't express it like her. If my love for you were a beautiful image, a work of art I can see clearly in my mind, then I was a sculptor with no hands; a painter with no eyes; a composer with no ears. Your mother is that emotional artist with great hands, keen eyes, and finely attuned ears.

" 'I was born looking inward—ideas excited me most. When I met your mom, I learned that so much of my inner life—a vast emotional landscape—had been hidden from me.

She is on solid footing on this terrain, she guided me. But I could only go so far. You sisters—you women—understand each other instinctively. I was outside that charmed circle, that triumvirate of female powers. My presence was often an intrusion, at times a provocation. Here I come, asking questions, making demands. How dare I presume rank?

I was a man and you were girls; certain gaps in understanding were inevitable. But the rest Mom helped to bridge.

" 'Sophia, after subjecting Mom to twenty-six hours of hard labor, you descended into our world, and ascended directly to the throne of our home. The work of delivering you foretold the demands you would make upon the world. You were like our first cat, Hero, who arrived at our home in a box I had carried from the ASPCA. He leapt out of the box and immediately declared himself lord and master. 'Where is my crown, where is my scepter?' he seemed to demand. Sophia, you expected the world to assemble before your throne, and it did. Your natural arrogance was a marvel, and a trial. Catherine the Great was not born with such natural *hauteur.* As much as it had to be countered, it also had to be admired.

" 'As you grew and faced real challenges and trials, your fiery confidence was tested. By putting you into doubt, these tests improved you, taught you humility and compassion. But never forget to be who you are. At bottom, do not doubt yourself. You are strong, yes, but also thoughtful and kind. People will always gravitate to someone with such force of character. People need you to be who you are, because people need a leader. Don't shrink from that.

" 'There are so many things I wanted to share with you, to discuss with you, to do with you. I feel such sadness now that I will miss those milestones of your life—your college graduation; your career and real independence; your wedding (should you choose to marry); your children (should you choose to be a mother). I should be there, I desperately want to be there, to show you how proud I am, a smitten father, so proud of his daughter. I desperately wanted to be there to witness these landmarks in your life. I am so very sad that I cannot.

" 'At each of these milestones, Sophia, remember to hold yourself to your own standards, not to those of society. Make your own choices. Always do what you think is necessary and right. Because you are very good, and your standards are higher than others'. Don't abandon those ideals—though you must sometimes compromise—because the world needs you, a woman of fortitude, of principles, of unbreakable will.

" 'Jane: you were blessed with the uninhibited freedom and confidence to say and do whatever you wanted. Because of that freedom, your originality always found easy expression. You fell from your mom's womb after only two hours of labor and I caught you myself. The ease of your birth portended the happiness of your childhood. It brought smiles to Mom and I, to our home, and from there, to the rest of the world.

" 'Your birth coincided, almost to the day, with the purchase of the old farm house upstate, which suited your natural wildness. You were a true *enfant sauvage*. Bear and deer, eagle and crow, fish and frog, salamander and snake—you embraced them as friends. When I first brought you a garter snake, your immediate instinct was to reach for it; when I first showed you the big black rat snake that lived by the pond, your first instinct was to grab it by the tail. You loved walking through the forest after the rain to collect salamanders. You spent countless hours by yourself wading in the pond, rain or shine, catching fish and frogs. Your connection to nature, like your connection to your inner nature, is strong: you must honor it and strengthen it. Trust your inner nature! It is your source of power.

" 'It is also the source of your creativity. We loved your 'bird cartoons' so much, not because of the art (which is still funny and original) but because of the hilarious situations you put those birds in. Perhaps you abandoned those drawings because we paid too much attention to them, or maybe we urged you too hard. But how we laughed! There is an artist or writer in you, and I predict your creativity will be a great source of happiness for you.

" 'Cultivate your natural athleticism. You have tremendous balance, coordination and strength. When I watched you earn your black belt in tae kwon do, I was so proud. Not for the belt, but to see how graceful and powerful—how *natural*—your moves were. I was so disappointed when you stopped. You and Sophia must know that physical culture is vital to personal growth, for many reasons you cannot yet see. But take my word for it, as you get older, it becomes more and more important. The essential thing is to lay down these habits now. Find a regular fitness routine. Each of you is blessed with a good strong body. It will turn against you if you don't take care of it.

" 'Jane and Sophia, only late in life did I learn the language of feelings, how to understand it, how to speak it. I hope these words convey—I hope you feel—how deep my love is for you. I've thought of you, hoped and dreamed for each of you in a thousand ways you cannot fathom. I've been surprised, frustrated, mystified, scorned, infuriated, and delighted by you. Without you, my daughters, I would only be half a man. With the first half I conceived you; with the second half I became your father. I would die without hesitation, so that you could live. But these feelings come naturally to fatherhood. Much harder was restructuring my life around you. Learning to put my children first, as long as it took, completed my education as a man. Now the payoff: knowing I helped you become who you are; helped reveal some of the possibilities within you; helped you dream and strive, to accept great challenges, and to try your utmost, though you may fail. If I helped you to that point, that is my reward as a father.

" 'Sometimes a father is needed by his children, even when they are adults. I feel a stabbing pain to think of those moments I won't be there for you. When those moments come, know that there is unlimited love and pride in my heart, something you may draw upon for the rest of your lives.

" 'Sophia and Jane, take care of Mom. She loves you beyond measure. She has poured her life into you. My most important relationship was with her. But *her* most important relationship is with you. She is the very meaning of devotion, the truest person you will ever know. Be as true to her as she is to you."

I was hunched forward in my chair, looking down at my notepad. A teardrop fell onto it, smearing the ink. If I had to say another word, the damned-up tears of my youth might have broken forth in a violent flood. But I didn't have to. I could see, as I looked around the room, that I had been understood.

Janáček delicately ended the group session.

"Gentlemen, you have done well. You treated this exercise with utmost seriousness and feeling. This will serve you and your loved ones well. Now we'll break for some refreshment, then have another round of one-on-one meetings, which will start in fifteen minutes. In the final group session, beginning around four o'clock, you will declare your Great Goal to the group. Use this time to reconsider your goal. If you do not feel an *inner necessity* to achieve this goal prior to your death, abandon it, and I will assign one to you."

Now the coach beckoned Anastas, the tall genial Dutchman, over to the open door leading down to the basement. He followed Janáček gamely, looking over his shoulder to the rest of us with a shrug and a grin that did not completely mask his concern. Lowering his head, he descended the basement stairs after one last look back.

I could not imagine the point of meeting in the basement. I had been down there before. It was an ancient dirt hollow holding Rich's wine collection, a furnace, a couple of bare light bulbs, and little else. There was no furniture, just dirt and darkness. What was going on down there? I looked over at Rich, turning my palms up in question. He betrayed no reaction whatsoever.

I grabbed a cup of coffee, and the Xerox copy Janáček had given me, and headed out to the deck. The fresh air and sunshine were a relief from Janáček's hard gaze, and all that talk of death.

After reading for ten or fifteen minutes, I heard the screen door creak open. Anastas appeared, with an ashen face and a blank, distant stare. He walked right past me, unseeing, as if I wasn't there. It looked like he had aged ten years. He stepped uncertainly into the yard, into the sunlight, and walked across the lawn. Where was he going?

Ten or fifteen minutes later the screen door squeaked opened again. As it closed with a *thwack*, I saw Evan, with a ghastly look and a thousand-yard stare, wander into the yard like an automaton, and across the lawn in the direction of the woods.

One after the other they emerged from the basement with the same ashen look and to a man they shuffled toward the light, none uttering a word or looking my way. By now I was more than curious—I was worried—about my meeting with the coach. Anxiously I awaited my turn.

I heard the screen door squeak open again; this time Janáček appeared.

"Mr. Donelan, are you ready?"

He immediately turned back into the house and went down the basement stairs. I followed. A few steps down from the kitchen, someone closed the door behind me. The darkness was profound. The damp air was oppressive and smelled like earth. Reaching the bottom stair, I saw ahead of me a dim light bulb dangling from a wire, and beyond that, the furnace. In an open room to the right I saw the criss-crossed wooden racks that held Rich's wine collection. To the left, I saw a flickering light coming from a gap in the wall, about thirty feet away.

"This way," called Janáček, and I walked slowly toward the light. Turning the corner, I saw him standing before an open coffin holding a candle. Without a word, he beckoned toward the coffin with one hand. I froze in terror. I could not move. I must have fainted then, because the next thing I knew I was in the coffin,. The silhouette of Janáček's head, bent over me, was back-lit by flickering candle light. He was reading an incantation, over and over again, with a hypnotizing rhythm. It sounded like ancient Greek but I had no idea what it meant:

"Το θεϊκό Brimo έχει γεννήσει το άγιο παιδί Brimos: ο ισχυρός έχει γεννήσει δύναμη. Το θεϊκό Brimo έχει γεννήσει το άγιο παιδί Brimos: ο ισχυρός έχει γεννήσει δύναμη. Το θεϊκό Brimo έχει γεννήσει το άγιο παιδί Brimos: ο ισχυρός έχει γεννήσει δύναμη."

Janáček's voice seemed to come from far away, as if he were calling from another world. I tried to cry out but was paralyzed, like in a nightmare when you can't move or scream. As he finished his incantation, he reached over me to pull down the coffin's lid.

Darkness blotted out my eyes, filled my nose and throat, compressed my heart and lungs. Death enfolded me in its stifling embrace. As the casket lid closed, I heard my screams explode in the sealed box. This is the last thing I remember before blacking out.

Chapter 6

Reprieve

I woke up in a sun-drenched bedroom, on an antique four-poster bed. The walls were painted luscious sage and grape colors. The windowsills and door frames were a radiant white. The curtains were a buttery yellow, the shades a rich purple. My eyes brimmed with light and color. Everything around me was brilliant and animated.

I must have fallen asleep in Rich's guest room. Like everything else in his life, it was sumptuous and tasteful. I looked out the window. The treetops swayed and danced in the wind. Their movement occupied my attention for some time. The world sought my eyes, clamored for my attention. Each thing called to me: *I am here for you, you are here for me!* Overnight, meaning had returned; beauty had returned. Desire and interest, value and meaning—all were restored. Suddenly, I was seized by a powerful sense of purpose, and I leaped out of bed.

I dressed quickly and ran downstairs to find Rich in the kitchen, drinking coffee. He didn't seem to recognize me. "What the hell? You're smiling for a change. Is it the old you? Maybe all you needed was a good night's sleep."

"How did I get upstairs?" I asked.

"You don't remember? Janáček left, everyone went home, you crashed here. You don't remember going to bed?"

"The last thing I remember, I was lying in that coffin. That was truly bizarre—and terrifying. What happened after that? Did someone carry me upstairs?"

Rich gave me a sympathetic and somewhat amused look. "Yeah, that was weird. I knew it was coming, but Janáček swore me to secrecy. The casket was delivered Friday, and a couple of guys with a van picked it up last night. You were freaked out by it, like everyone else but maybe a little bit more. You came upstairs, dazed and confused, like the rest of us. We all sat on the porch, trying to absorb that experience. Janáček suggested wine. We had quite a few bottles. You're telling me you don't remember any of this?" Rich asked incredulously.

I searched my memory, but the last thing I could recall was Janáček chanting and closing the coffin over my head.

"And what happened in the final group session?"

"What do you mean?" Rich said. "Everyone shared their goals and pledged to complete them in one year. You were there and you were participating fully. " Now he gave me a look of concern.

"Did I drink three bottles of wine or something? Did I have a stroke? How could I possibly forget all that?"

Rich's look of concern intensified. "Wow, you are serious," he said.

"Did I pledge my goal, the marathon?"

"What? No man, that is *my* goal." Rich looked at me queerly. "Your goal is to write a book."

"A book? What kind of book? Did I say anything about it?"

"No, but when you declared it, the strangest thing happened. Janáček smiled, like a human being. A big, beautiful smile. It was kind of eerie, like he was hoping you'd say that."

To which I replied, "Weird."

Rich continued: "Janáček loosened up a little after that, though not going so far as to smile a second time. After the second glass of wine he became animated—well, at least for a stiff like him—and regaled us with Cold War stories. You fell asleep on the couch. I woke you up, pointed you to the bedroom...and that was it." He paused then took a sip of his coffee. "Maybe you did have a stroke. Seriously."

Maybe this was true, but right now it didn't matter. For the first time in many months, I knew exactly what to do. It was perfectly clear. I had to get back to the city to start writing my book. But what book had I committed to writing? I had no idea. What I knew was that I *had* to do it. Janáček was right—it felt, as he put it, "subjectively necessary".

Just then, as if struck by lightning, I knew what the book would be about. It was obvious: it would be about this experience. I would write about the transformative power of the Great Goal—and how it restored meaning to my life. This book would be *my* Great Goal. Nice, simple, clear.

I had to leave, *now.* I didn't know whether my new lease on life, so full of promise, would last forever or dry up in a few hours.

I stood up, drained my coffee cup, and thanked Rich profusely.

"Rich, I can't say what happened, but I can't thank you enough. Somehow, you knew this was exactly what I needed. Everything is different today. Janáček...what a pompous ass! But he knows things. He somehow got into my head. Whatever he did, I now have a purpose, I now know what to do. If it wasn't for you, I would still be wandering aimlessly in melancholia. I'm so grateful. Really. You can't imagine. Thanks, bro. And now, I gotta go."

We traded hugs, and I bolted through the front door and hopped into the minivan. I drove out of the woods and found my way back to the county road. But before turning onto it, I rolled down the window and gazed in wonder at the brilliant clouds rushing past a pure azure sky. The treetops danced in the wind. I knew exactly what to do. Not just now, but tomorrow, and the next day, too.

Had Janáček, that pompadoured prima donna, flipped a switch in my head? He had grasped my state of mind with uncanny speed and clarity. He had seen something in me, something desperate perhaps. He had found—or implanted—in me an *inner necessity.*

As I turned on to the Thruway, a Doors song came on the radio. Morrison warned:

"Keep your eyes on the road, your hands upon the wheel!"

I moved to the left lane, accelerated to traffic speed, and my inner autopilot took over. But before long, in my rearview mirror, a blue BMW pulled up fast and close, flashing his headlights. I'm doing eighty—and he's right up my ass... damned annoying. But I'm hemmed in on the right and I can't move over to let him pass.

"Let it roll, baby roll, let it roll..."

On the other side of the concrete median, just a few feet to my left, the oncoming traffic whizzed past. An eighteen-wheeler was coming up fast, hugging the barrier, its trailer rocking noticeably. *Why is that truck in the fast lane?* I thought. Suddenly a shower of sparks rose up behind it, and then a black shape rose over the median, coming right at me, darkening my view. I raised my left arm instinctively for protection and hit the brake hard—but instead, I stomped on the gas pedal, and the car lurched violently forward. In the rear-view mirror, I saw the giant truck tire slam into the BMW's windshield. The car skidded sideways, rolled over, then *boom!—boom!* Two cars hit it in succession at full speed.

Do I stop? I asked myself, aghast. The traffic behind the totaled BMW ground to a halt. I pulled away with the rest of the pack, the trailing edge of life recoiling from death for now. *Poor guy! How could he have survived that?* I clutched the wheel and tried to compose myself, exhaling deeply. Only then did I hear the Doors song winding down. From far away Morrison intoned:

"The future's uncertain, the end is always near".

I must have been lost in thought for the next forty-five minutes because the next thing I saw was the George Washington Bridge, the Hudson River, and fabulous Manhattan, glittering in the sun. The woven steel cables of the bridge glinted against a cloudless blue sky. Sunlight reflected from the sails of the boats below. These flashes of sunlight signaled beauty and purpose like semaphores. I knew without a doubt what I had to do.

It was early Sunday, not yet noon. I wasn't expected home until evening, so I decided to go straight to my office to write. I had no time to waste. I could not let this feeling of urgency pass. The crash had rattled me hard. But I knew I had to start *now.* I parked in the Village and walked to my office in Chelsea. Today, I would break ground on my Great Goal.

Chapter 7

Wishing

My laptop, dark with inactivity, sat inert on the conference table. I couldn't concentrate. The car crash replayed over and over in my head. *Why him?* If I had braked, it would have been me. I'd be dead now. Had that driver drawn *my* lottery ticket? Was it *my* fate to die like that? Or was it my fate to see *him* die like that?

I couldn't write a word, so I got up and wandered over to the windows looking down on Twenty-Sixth Street. This street had changed drastically in the last fifteen years. The grimy, worn down commercial blocks in the twenties between Fifth and Tenth Avenue were no place to be on the weekends. In the early '90s, they were still lined with ancient garment industry shops (selling buttons, spools, scissors, sewing machines). Back then, there were still a few sweatshops. Madison Square Park was prowled by hookers and dime-bag dealers. Plastic crack vials crunched underfoot. The benches were broken, or their planks removed to stop the homeless from sleeping there. The monuments looked insulted. But today, unbelievably, the park has been restored, and the street were now lively and clean (for New York City anyway). Taxis and Ubers ferried guests to and from the hotel across the street. Tourists and day-trippers were everywhere.

Across the street, a trophy mom stalked past, pushing a kid in a two thousand-dollar stroller, her nanny in tow. Further down the street, a cluster of jocks (or former jocks) lined up in front of a sports bar to watch the World Series. The speed of change in Manhattan—the turnover of buildings and shops, the scaffolding and construction crews, the migration of people and businesses—reminded me that one day I would also be absorbed into its past.

Time flew. But instead of enjoying this beautiful day with my wife and kids, I was in an unlit conference room, praying for the opening sentence of my book. *How will they remember me when I am gone*? I wondered. *As a father who pursued selfish goals at the expense of time with them?* Vanity of vanities! The thought of Sophia and Jane riding their bikes along the waterfront without me was painful. *Their childhood will soon be over. I should rush outside and celebrate life—while it lasts!*

But I felt I had no choice. I needed to create something lasting. If it was ever going to happen, it was now. I couldn't quite explain it, I just knew this was my last chance to do something great.

I had dinner last week in Chinatown and found this message in my fortune cookie:

"Great souls have wills; feeble ones only have wishes."

It hit me viscerally, like an accusation. Was I just a dreamer, a feeble soul? Or did I have the willpower to accomplish my goal, whatever the obstacles? The question seized my heart with doubt...but beneath this tremor I felt a deep thrill, a sense of risk and excitement. I had to see this through. I had to write my book. But how?

Some are born, it seems, with great goals and an unshakeable conviction to see them through. Like Joan of Arc or Mahatma Gandhi, they have a calling, an inborn vocation. History sometimes matches a great person to a universal human need, like Euclid and geometry, Newton and gravity, Marie Curie and radiation. Their role in history seems assigned by fate. They are sometimes thought mad—like Mallory, who thought he was fated to conquer Everest, and Hillary, who finally did it. They are often obsessives with outsized, unreasonable goals, like Elon Musk in our time.

With the blessing of their talent—and their indomitable will to achieve greatness—they were given something else quite valuable: a meaningful life.

Others—most of us—are not so lucky; we must actively seek our sources of meaning and purpose. As post-modern adults we grasp, if reluctantly, that the meaning we derive as individuals from natural laws and social rules and conventions is insufficient for us to justify our lives. Rather, we must construct, as individuals, our own meaning, including the purpose of our life. We must also learn to avert our eyes from the void of meaninglessness that periodically threatens to swallow us up.

Suddenly, I remembered: I once tried something great—my master's thesis. It was on Kant's Critique of Judgment. I never finished it and I still can't say why. What had happened, so many years ago? What went wrong? I remember researching furiously, reading and rereading primary sources, then secondary sources, then commentary and commentary on commentary. I cross-referenced, annotated and indexed. But I could never shake the feeling that I *needed to know more* before

I could start writing. I needed more information. I attempted the opening paragraph forty times, but this thought stopped me. Each attempt felt wrong. I felt totally unqualified.

The final form of my thesis—five or six legal pads full of notes and drafts—was in a box in my attic upstate. That box of legal pads was a permanent tribute to my failure, which now stirred painfully in its grave. Why had I failed? It made no sense. I had great teachers, I did all the reading. I had the support of my advisor. I had my trusty *MLA Handbook*. But something went horribly wrong—I couldn't write a word.

I closed my laptop, locked the office and took the elevator down to the street. Walking, I immediately feel better.

I reenter the bloodstream of the city. I am borne along by its lifeblood, the people. Pedestrians, construction crews, drivers, cops, families, celebrities, tourists, and dogs of all kinds. If sidewalk traffic stops, the blood-flow reroutes automatically, flowing around obstacles, like a stream around a rock. Some work along its banks, hawking goods from folding tables. Some try to save my soul with pamphlets. Some try to sell me a monthly subscription which will save children's lives. I wander without conscious purpose. I cross paths with taxis, food trailers, bicycles, scooters, skateboards, strollers. My feet carry me along with no assistance from the so-called higher functions. There are a fixed number of paths on the grid between my office and home, and my feet know them all. With my body on autopilot, my mind is free to wander.

Soon I recall a scene from the distant past. I was in grad school, at NYU's Bobst Library, struggling with my thesis. Emerging from a fourth-floor study room—one of those white, windowless cubicles that are supposed to minimize distraction—I wandered instinctively toward the light streaming into the tall clerestory windows facing Washington Square Park.

Looking out, I spied tender buds in the treetops, eye level to me. The warmth and promise of spring had finally arrived, and people naturally sought a place in the sun.

A juggler performed in the fountain, still dry this time of year. Tourists, students, and random passers-by sat around the fountain with their legs dangling in, soaking up the sun. Near the Arch, some latter-day hippies gathered around a duo of folk guitarists. Solitary young men wandered the paths without apparent purpose, but everyone knows they are selling weed. Older folks sat on benches along the walkways, reading newspapers or doing a crossword. Late risers held blue, Greek-themed coffee cups with the slogan WE ARE HAPPY TO SERVE YOU. Some fed squirrels, some gazed at the budding trees, some idly watched these various scenes playing out before them.

I forced myself back into the study room. But as I sat, its unbroken white walls became a projection screen for my restless imagination. Before long I am soaring over a mountainous South American jungle—endless, impenetrable, mysterious. Just beneath the jungle canopy a column of Spanish soldiers are hacking their way through dense undergrowth. It is an expedition to El Dorado, led by the brutal conquistador Aquirre [5].

His soldiers attempt to cross a treacherous river, but every attempt fails. Finally they build a raft of logs, and try to ferry it across with a rope guideline. But in the first attempt, the raft is torn away with two men on it. It is tossed on the rapids and then caught in a whirlpool, turning endlessly. The men cannot be reached from shore. If they jump off, they will drown. Before long one, and then the other, falls to the deck, overwhelmed by vertigo. An awful fate awaits them—they will never leave that raft.

But the conquistador Aguirre is unmoved. Indeed, he is annoyed. Yet another hindrance! With implacable, dead-eyed certainty, he overcomes every obstacle standing in his way. The jungle is no match for the monstrous force of Aguirre's will. He sees no reason for delay. He orders his party upstream, in search of a better crossing, leaving the two soldiers spinning to their deaths.

The rhythmic beeping of a truck in reverse breaks through my reverie and reminds me I am walking home. I find myself turning left on to Eighth Avenue. Why did I fail at my thesis? Suddenly it was clear. I'm a dreamer. Like a dreamer, I had dodged the hard necessity of the will—the necessity of writing with a fixed deadline. Dreaming had undermined my goal, and I had let it happen. Without a doubt, there was something to this. I enjoyed dreaming so much more than writing.

Freud claimed that desires are satisfied in part by involuntary processes like wishing and dreaming. But wishing for or dreaming about a goal brings us no closer to it. On the contrary, wishing seems to *discharge* desire in some measure, diminishing its intensity, and offering temporary satisfaction along the steep rocky path to the goal. It provides *catharsis*—a surrogate fulfillment that relieves the pressure of desire if only momentarily. In 1976, President Jimmy Carter confessed in an interview with *Playboy* magazine that he had sinned in his heart. But this kind of "sinning" might have saved him from sin. If wishing discharges the tension of the will, purposeful action is *less* likely to arise.

If the thought is not equal to the deed, even less is the wish. A wish does not require the validation of becoming 'real". Instead wishing, experienced inwardly, is a living phenomenon valid in its own right, requiring no rationale, intention, or purpose. Its function for the psyche is very different from that of the will. Willing always has an object or end, while wishing is valuable just *because* it lacks an intentional object. Willing attempts to resolve desire; wishing tends to perpetuate it.

So contrary to the wisdom of the Chinese proverb, wishing is *not* an inferior form of willing. Wishing cannot be ginned up into an act of will. These two forms of desire are not part of a continuous spectrum; rather, they are categorically different. Wishing is private, subjective, and fulfills unconscious needs; whereas willing is public, objective, and fulfills conscious needs. Wishing is valid in its own right and should not be diminished by comparison to willing. But how do I prevent wishing and dreaming from undermining my willpower and compromising my Great Goal?

Walking west on Gansevoort Street, I realized these thoughts might be the starting point for my book. I picked up my pace, was home in a few minutes, and immediately sat down to write whatever I could recall.

Chapter 8

Dreaming

I pledged to myself I would get up early each morning, write for an hour, then do the same thing when I got home at night. But morning after morning, night after night, though I forced myself to the writing chair, I could not make myself write. The pressure of the will seemed hostile to the act of writing.

One day, I noticed that ideas for the book flowed freely when walking to and from work. So the next morning, instead of writing, I left the apartment early and walked slowly to work. I walked up Ninth Avenue, at some point turned east, and by alternate uptown and crosstown streets found my way to my office in Chelsea. As I walked, unburdened by the pressure to write, images rose up in a strong, continuous flow. Images of my childhood appeared, and with them, images of my father.

Cancer took my father last year. I thought of him often now. I recalled a scene from my childhood in the New Jersey suburbs. It was 1971, and I had been grounded to my room. In those days "grounding" was a new and enlightened form of punishment, an alternative to spanking. It consisted of forcing a ten-year old boy to do what he cannot possibly do—stay confined in one place. For my strict Catholic parents, grounding was never the only punishment, just a supplemental one. Spankings were still *de rigueur* at home and at Catholic school. But spanking didn't deter me much. It didn't take long for me to learn that it hurt for a little while, then it didn't. Thus other forms of torment, like being forced to write "I will take out the trash" five hundred times, were needed. Eventually no form of punishment worked on me. But they had to do something, so they settled on incarceration.

It was probably more painful for my parents to keep me indoors than to send me out. They were loving parents, but they were principled to a fault. They had no choice but to keep their word, especially when it came to punishment. Thus I was consigned to long periods of solitude, sequestered from the world for days—and sometimes weeks—at a time. Nor was it likely I would secure early release. Principled to a fault, you see.

I was not so much an unruly child as a normal ten-year-old boy. But I lived in a house in which baseline behavior was defined by a super-disciplined mother and my four sisters, her faithful adjutants. By their measure, my behavior was outrageous, off the charts. My mere presence was a provocation.

Back then, dad traveled a lot on business, and Mom, left alone with five kids and her principled refusal to compromise, suffered greatly. She did not hesitate to spank (though as I grew, spanking hurt her hand too much, so she switched a wooden spoon). But as I mentioned, spanking no longer deterred me. Infraction piled upon infraction. My mom tracked my violations closely, but even she lost count. I was constantly threatened with that cliché of consequences: "Wait 'til your father gets home!"

So when my dad got home from his business trips, rather than running to greet him, I was more likely to run upstairs to my bedroom. Eventually, he settled in and sat down to a kitchen table conference with my mom, who presented the litany of my crimes. I pressed my ear closely to the air duct in my bedroom floor, just above the kitchen, to listen as my fate was pronounced.

Mom presented her case. "Peter, this week was a nightmare. Right after you left, Andrew broke a garage door window with the basketball. The next day, I guess it was Sunday, he left the gate open and the dog got out. I sent him out to search for Holly on his bike but it was many hours before she returned home. Holly is in heat, of course, and I'm sure every male in the neighborhood had his way with her. Guaranteed we get a litter of mutts in the spring.

"Anyway, Monday he left his brand-new raincoat on the bus. Tuesday he got detention for talking back to Sister Patricia. He says she picked him up by his ears and carried him to the principal's office. God bless Sister Patricia! Then Wednesday afternoon I got a call from the school nurse. I was resting after lunch, watching Days of Our Lives—the only break I get during the day! The nurse said he gashed his head playing tackle football in the parking lot and I had to come pick him up. Of course, he was fine, not much blood and no reason to send him home. Thursday he left his bike in the street and June Allen ran it over. Of course she drives like a maniac, but still it was his fault. Then yesterday after dinner he threw a basketball at Glenn Roachford's head and knocked him out flat on his driveway. Glenn's mom ran over here, screaming hysterically—and drunk, as usual—while Glenn lay in her driveway, apparently dead. A few minutes later he must have woken up, because the boys ran back over here, took her by the hand and walked her home.

Oh yeah, he refused, he *blatantly refused,* to take the trash cans out to the street. So yesterday we missed the pickup. The only damned responsibility he has, and now all the trash cans are full."

Her words, as I heard them, were distorted by the heating duct, giving them a hollow, oracular sound. I pressed my ear to the grate, and remained motionless, an anxious supplicant awaiting the oracle's judgement. What would be my fate? Finally the conference ended, and before long I heard the creaking of stairs as Dad climbed stealthily up to my room. I knew a spanking was coming, possibly the belt. Buy I also knew he had to do it and he didn't want to, so I forgave him in advance. He was a very reluctant enforcer. He was torn between his duty to Mom and his sympathy for me.

Admittedly, it had not been a great year for me. In June, I had started a fire in the woods at the end of the street. It's too late now to credibly claim it was an accident, but it really was. Glenn Roachford and I carried an empty mayonnaise jar into the woods behind Glenn's house, filled it with dry oak leaves, then threw in a lighted match. In no time the jar was too hot to hold—ten-year-old boys are very easily surprised—so I dropped it, as luck would have it, on a rock. We stomped furiously on the fire until it spread in every direction. It wasn't long before two noisy, self-satisfied fire trucks arrived, disgorging shouting bands of firemen. They quickly put out the fire then carried Glenn and I, by hands and feet, to our homes. They deposited my crumpled, smoking figure on the porch and rang the doorbell. My father opened the front door, trying his best to look surprised. When the firemen left, Dad said, "Son, if you tell me the truth, I won't spank you. Did you start the fire?"

"No."

Grounded again! Thus punishment multiplied upon punishment.

One Saturday in September—for no good reason—I threw an apple at a neighbor cutting his lawn, the next block over. I ran away in plain sight, apparently believing I was invisible. The neighbor complained to my dad. He knew just who I was, and on top of that, he was a cop. Among the many things I did not know.

Dad said I had to apologize personally, like a man. He walked me to the end of the cop's driveway and forced me to take the long perp walk, alone, to the front door. Behind the screen the cop's hulking silhouette watched my cowering advance. On top of this humiliation, I was grounded yet again, every day after school for a month. My punishments multiplied, and I could see no way out.

As my grief and anger from this month-long punishment grew, I became a raging, caged animal. At some point a fiber in my brain must have snapped. I had to escape! I finally attempted it one beautiful October evening. It was on a Friday after dinner, and there was still a little light left in the sky. The night was cool and crisp, but the last traces of summer warmth still lingered in the air. The sound of my sisters and friends playing outside goaded me beyond all restraint. I popped out my window screen, and stepped out onto the roof of the garage. I climbed down and was promptly caught. All my time served was erased, and my entire sentence began again. I howled in frustration and pain, knowing there would be no reprieve.

During my earliest incarcerations, books were the only alternative to total boredom. The bookcase in my room was not really mine, but a common repository for the family's discarded literature. There were trashy best sellers, a dictionary, a Bible, some illustrated adventure books, and stacks of old magazines. There were several issues of *Highlights*, the Christian kids' magazine, deadly boring even for a ten-year-old. *Highlights* featured a comic strip called "Gufus and Gallant." Gufus was unruly and rude, while Gallant was improbably decent and well-mannered. I understood that he was supposed to be a model Christian lad. But I saw him as a gutless, brown-nosing conformist. Because they went too far with Gallant's virtues, I came to identify more with Gufus. He was a jerk, but at least he was an individual.

Fortunately, I also had *How and Why Wonder Books* on my shelf. I must have read these illustrated science magazines a hundred times, committing to memory the Latin names of dinosaurs and sharks, birds and insects. Eventually, I put them aside and turned to the illustrated adventure stories—abridged editions, in an oversized hardcover format—including *Moby Dick, The Call of the Wild,* and *20,000 Leagues Under the Sea*. As a rule, they contained one illustration per chapter—a key metric for a ten-year-old boy. Eventually I moved on to whatever else had pictures, like my mom's old sewing magazines, and even the sewing machine manual itself (featuring line drawings of the machine). Then I turned to the *Merriam-Webster's Dictionary* (which featured little drawings next to certain words). I had almost reached the letter B, when I turned my attention to a blue cloth–bound book with gold lettering, the Holy Bible.

I started with the Scriptures—not because my parents were devout Catholics, but because when I flipped through the book's silver-edged pages, I found passages with red letters, and zeroed in on those. I worked my way backward from the scriptures to the stories of the Old Testament—Adam and Eve, Abraham and Isaac, Esau and Jacob, Ezekiel, Jonah, Job.

Finally, some wayward American classics had found their way to my bookcase. They were imposing tomes with cloth bindings, *Modern Library* editions probably bought at a yard sale. I found *The Scarlet Letter, The Last of the Mohicans, The Collected Tales and Poems of Edgar Allen Poe,* and read them one after the other in my drive to systemically account for every word on that bookshelf.

My physical circumstances were unchanging. But inwardly there was constant change, a sense of novelty and excitement, in whatever stories were in my hand. In my exile all that dammed-up prepubescent energy was channeled into thoughts and images, branching rapidly in every direction. Each new idea struck roots. Gradually, my exile became an enchanted refuge, my own Neverland. Solitude and boredom were my gateway to a private dreamworld in which imagination was sovereign.

Outside my room, I was an active—maybe hyperactive—boy. A heedless pup, trying everything, pulling things down, fouling the carpets, getting into every conceivable mischief. I could expend my energy in action. But locked in my room, I could not. My imagination ran wild, but my hands were tied. Had my will—that muscle connecting thought and action—atrophied? Had it gotten weak and flabby from disuse? Was willpower my Achilles' heel?

I looked up to find myself in front of my office building. I hurried upstairs, went directly to the conference room and wrote down whatever I could remember.

Chapter 9

Willing

Janáček mentioned a little book by Schopenhauer,[6] so after work I took a detour to the Strand Book Store on Broadway and Twelfth Street, and easily found it there, used, for $11.00.

What is the will? To explain, Schopenhauer draws a sharp distinction between wishing and willing. He claims wishing is "not even resolve, much less volition."[7] He also states that two contrary wishes present no contradiction to the mind. In fact, with no sense of contradiction, we may even wish for the impossible.

But willing (volition) is very different. In contrast to wishing, we can only will one thing at a time. For example, fasting. As long as I will to fast, it prevents me from eating; but if I choose to eat, this cancels the prior volition.[8] I may fast or eat, but I cannot do both. When the will is presented with conflicting intentions, motives and counter-motives clash, but only one of them survives to become a volition.

Suddenly—I can't say how—I feel a firm determination to *do* something. I feel an impetus to action—without knowing what the action should be. A general sense that *something* should be done— a feeling of resolve—carries me to the doorstep of volition. But crossing the threshold from resolve to action requires a radical narrowing of possibilities. It requires an act of exclusion called decision. The Latin root of this word (*decidere*) means "to cut off". It shares a common root with suicide, homicide, pesticide, and so on. Decision is a *killing off* of alternate choices, alternate futures.[9] By an act of radical exclusion, decision turns resolve into action.

We can never know enough to act with *total* certainty. We might always become more informed, and critical new information might appear tomorrow. Uncertainty and risk might "rationally" keep us forever from acting. But despite a fundamental uncertainty, the will takes the risk. Out of the flux of sense, out of the tumult of conflicting motives, the will seizes upon just one thing. It plucks meaning from chaos. It steps boldly into the uncertain and changes the world.

The will's intense focus heightens the distinction of the self from the object, which in turn heightens desire. In contrast to wishing, willing engages—and often conflicts with—the physical world and the ethical world. Because it is specific and action-oriented, the will can accomplish great things. But it can also cause great harm, bringing social condemnation and even legal punishment.

Though I lack the strength and discipline, I *will* write my book. Though I fear it is beyond my ability, I *must* write my book. Only now do I see, with painful clarity, the consequences of this decision. There are a thousand reasons why I might not. But I feel, against every objective reason, that it is *necessary* for me. The decision has been made. I have killed off alternative futures. I will make whatever sacrifice is necessary.

On the island of the Lotus Eaters, the crew of Odysseus ate the Lotus fruit and became intoxicated. They sank into a listless dream state, helpless to act of their own accord. Only Odysseus could resist the temptation, and ignore the pathetic pleas of the Lotus Eaters to forget about home and join their beautiful dream. They could not shake the resolve of the wily King of Ithaca.

Resolute Odysseus, be my model! I must depart from this Island of Dreams! I must abandon its warmth, its sunny skies, its narcotic fruit. As Odysseus commanded his men, I command my body! Despite the late hour, the rising swells, the darkening sky—today I put my boat on the waves. Today I face the rigors of the will.

Chapter 10

Commitment

Months have passed since I set out on the dark sea of my Great Goal. Every day I fight the wind and waves driving me back from my goal and from the daily discipline of writing. It's April now, and I arrive home on a Thursday after work, around 6:30. It's a mild, lovely evening and everyone is outside, celebrating the return of spring. The annual tulip festival is underway in Abingdon Square Park, just outside my window. On the other side of Hudson Street, Bleecker Street Park is full of young children and their doting parents. High-pitched shrieks of delight periodically pierce the air. The cafes and restaurants are packed; the sidewalks bustle with energy. Along the waterfront, people line the park benches and look out over the Hudson River at the setting sun.

It's painful to be inside on such a beautiful evening. The work week is almost over, the weekend lies ahead. The darkness and cold of winter has passed. It's one of those moments that make living in Manhattan worthwhile, a moment to be savored. But with a sinking heart, I turn my back on this beauty. I reject this pleasure to satisfy the harsh demands of the will. I have pledged to write. Like every day at this time I am seized by uncertainty. Every day is a another test. Will it ever get easier? Will I never be free of doubt? Will I ever find the mechanical, unquestioned conviction I need to write every day?

In mythology, world-changing events are often depicted as the monumental acts of gods and heroes, like Alexander cutting the Gordian knot. But among mortals, great things are never achieved in one stroke. For example, the notion of the author creating a sublime work of art in one tremendous act of inspiration is a myth. And what is that myth? That only great passion can achieve great goals. The importance of passion is largely overstated by motivational speakers and writers. Passion may be necessary to start something great—but it is not sufficient to achieve it. One must be passionate, by all means. The problem is that passion—an outburst of feeling—cannot be sustained. Passion tires of regular work. Thus many great goals, begun in a passion, are left by the roadside. Myths may depict great accomplishments as a single, monumental act. In fact, the greatest acts of will are sustained over a long time.

How do we turn a passionate decision to act into the countless steps needed to achieve a great goal? Repetition. But repetition a certain number of times will not do. Repetition that never expects to cease has a name: commitment. Commitment swears, in effect, to infinite repetition of the initial act of will. Without commitment, the greatest goals—long, difficult, and often doubtful—could never be achieved.

Commitment spares us the anguish of continuous doubt by waiving further deliberation. If we occasionally go out jogging, a deliberate act of will is required each time. But if we run regularly, little or no willpower is required each time. The committed regard the *reasons* for commitment as a settled matter. Commitment waives deliberation—i.e., further choice—and reflexively affirms the goal, again and again. Inwardly, it is felt as an unquestioned imperative: *I must do this.*

The effort of commitment is more like a marathon than a sprint. Commitment tests the endurance of the will more than its strength. In contrast to passion, commitment is rarely visible, and is demonstrated not in loud showy actions but quietly over time. Time is the proper medium of commitment because its method is not inspiration, but repetition. Because of its resistance to doubt, commitment is secular devotion. Commitment is constancy itself.

Commitment ignores "alternatives". Indeed commitment ignores facts. It sees the world in binary terms, as either/or. Either I am committed or I am not. Commitment is not "reasonable", for it rejects other possibilities in advance. This is brilliantly expressed in Nike's motto "Just do it"—which means in effect "stop thinking." Against options and alternatives that may tempt us, commitment reflexively re-affirms the goal as *necessary*. In effect, commitment deliberately limits individual freedom.

A decision without risk or sacrifice engenders no commitment. An alcoholic, avoiding the decision to quit, may take refuge in the thought that he can overcome alcoholism without giving up alcohol. He does not want either/or—he wants both. This kind of rationalizing "and"–type thinking wants the new thing and the old one too. Another word for "and" thinking is *hedging*. In the financial world, hedging is the systematic mitigation of risk; in the moral world, it is the continuous evasion of sacrifice.

The power of commitment rests on subjective, not objective, grounds. It rests on values, not on facts. Its logic is not mathematical but moral. It focuses not on net gain, but on what is *necessary*. For commitment is, at bottom, not *to* an object or goal, or even *to* another person. Commitment, at bottom, is to oneself. I declared to myself alone that I will write my book—and so I must. I cannot hedge this position, since I am at once defendant, judge, jury, and executioner.

Chapter 11

Distraction

Every day I struggled to honor my commitment to write. But two powerful forces—distraction and procrastination—opposed me. By very different but equally insidious means, distraction and procrastination constantly undermined the necessity I assigned to my goal, thereby reducing the likelihood of action. Distraction can be understood as an external or "objective" barrier to commitment; while procrastination can be seen as an internal or "subjective" barrier to commitment.

Distraction has a Latin root meaning "drawing apart," or "drawing away". Something secondary draws our focus away from our primary intent. Common language often refers to objects or circumstances or people as distractions. Distractions often arise out of the immediate environment, but also, independently, from thoughts, feelings, and memories. Few things are more distracting than powerful emotions, for example. Thus we can't conquer distraction merely by making changes to our environment, because even with blindfolds and a straightjacket on, inner distraction remains.

Without a doubt, the best defense against distraction is a clear sense of purpose. But no matter how clear the purpose may be, if the goal is difficult enough, doubts and anxieties will appear. It is in these moments that distraction poses the greatest threat.

For example, at the end of my workday, so full of challenges, frustrations and setbacks, I tried to avoid distractions and walk directly home. I tried to keep my head down until I achieved my daily milestone—to write from six-thirty to eight o'clock. I walked home from Chelsea to the West Village by many different routes. At every moment, at every turn, there were myriad opportunities for distraction. There were innumerable things to see, people to meet, stops to make. Assaulted at each step by a barrage of stimuli, spanning a spectrum from beautiful to repugnant, from delightful to awful—I averted my eyes. I turned my inner eye to the goal. But how could this goal, still so intangible, so difficult and remote, hold my attention amid the tumult and excitement of the city's streets?

I often walked my dog Juno to work. But this meant I also had to walk her home—an added hurdle on the way to the writing chair. At the end of the day I was hell-bent on getting home to write–but since Juno was a puppy she had to sniff every spot on the sidewalk and play with every dog she saw. So I'd loosen the leash a little for her, and for myself.

Dogs exert a civilizing force, drawing their masters together in a common sentiment, if only for a few minutes. They provide a solid pretext for benign social interaction, which in any case can hardly be avoided. Dogs pull dog owners together, who must exchange greetings and ask about the other dog, and from there, perhaps, ask polite questions about the other person. This happens many times a day, to and from work. Of course (I say to myself) my goal is first, I must stay true to it. But I'm no misanthrope. What's the point of living in Manhattan if I want to avoid people?

Leaving work around six o'clock, we headed down Seventh Avenue. Juno immediately spotted Jim, a guy who sells albums in front of the Radio Shack at the corner of Twenty-Third Street who has become a friend. He sits on a folding chair and greets every dog that comes by. Juno loves Jim, and drags me across the avenue to see him. She's forty pounds, but crawls into his lap like a lap dog. It's a love affair I can't deny her. Jim's a sidewalk philosopher and social theorist. He and I could talk for hours. But I rein it in, I limit myself to small talk—though not without a twinge of regret. We keep moving down Seventh.

Now Juno is yanking me hard down Twenty-First Street. I see a little black and white dog on the bottom step of a townhouse. I look up and realize it's a friend of mine sitting on the stoop with his daughter, just home from college. We chat, our dogs sniff and play, we have a few laughs and pledge to get together for dinner. I press onward.

Some shops put out dog biscuits, and Juno knows the location of every one in Chelsea. Shopkeepers know the dogs will pull you there. Only by advanced planning can I route her around these stores. But I don't really want to deprive her of a biscuit, or the attention she gets from the store clerks and customers. They seem to enjoy it. Certainly, Juno is a damn cute dog. It's definitely not *my* appeal that brings young women to their knees on the sidewalk, fussing and cooing and kissing Juno. This happens all the time, and I have nothing against it because I love my dog. Small talk ensues; we linger for a few minutes. Dogs are a social adhesive.

It was nearly six-thirty now; almost home. Walking west on Jane Street, I saw people on folding chairs, facing a storefront window, cheering, backslapping. What's this? The World Cup—a neighborhood tradition. The café owners of

Bonsignour are soccer fans, and every four years they put out chairs for everyone to watch the finals. Several of my neighbors are hanging around, cheering their teams. Juno is petted and loved all around. With each encounter, chitchat is required, but also enjoyed. The owner of the restaurant right next door comes out with two pitchers of beer—his team just scored. I sit and watch the game, drink a beer, and stay a little longer.

What is distraction, and why does it have such power? In its simplest form, distraction is just the attention continuously demanded by our senses. Our sensory organs are evolved to be attuned to danger. They generate instinctive responses so powerful that all other input is ignored. In the face of compelling sensations—not merely the fight-or-flight variety, but merely bright light, or loud sounds, or rapid movement—even the most forceful ideas and intentions evaporate. Those crystal–clear plans fade from view, becoming a mere shadowy outline. Our firm sense of conviction and control slackens; the richness of sense pours in to fill this vacuum. Our bodies becomes busy with activity, and the idea is all too easily eclipsed.

Before long though, recalling the *idea of the goal,* the will reawakens and reasserts itself. Recalling the goal seems to incite self-consciousness, or what Schopenhauer calls the will. The will sees the idea as an object it can attain. The idea of the goal is a mental, rather than visceral, standard for action when instinct and intuition are insufficient. The goal, as an idea, appears to be a unitary object of the will. But in fact, the will simultaneously grasps the idea of the goal, the self willing the goal, and the gap between them. The idea of the goal incites the will to close that gap, thereby providing purpose and meaning.

But the idea does not by itself produce action. In other words, it's not an immediate object to act on, but just a reflection. For action to occur the object must be chosen. The will does not merely perceive the gap between the self and the goal; it must attempt to close it. If this does not occur, then sense-life resumes control. A car horn honks; someone calls your name; your stomach grumbles with hunger. Without conscious intent, we are drawn back into the world of sense.

But the net effect of turning our attention from reflection back to sense is not a suspension of the goal. On the contrary, if we were not drawn away by the senses to engage with the world, we would accomplish nothing. Re-immersion in sense is a precondition for achieving the goal. It must be implemented by hands, by work. Thus we must re-immerse into sense-life, but in a way that is periodically checked by the idea.

Indeed, in moments of deeply immersive activity, what often interrupts us is not sense distraction but the idea. Am I conforming to the idea of the goal? Am I falling short? The idea of the goal often breaks the spell of total engagement, or "flow". In other words, sometimes the *idea* itself is the distraction.

In sum, distraction from the goal is neither the interruption of sense nor the intrusion of the idea, but rather the constant switching from one to the other—from the richness, diversity, and fluidity of sense, to the unity and simplicity of the idea—and then back again. Distraction is the failure to sustain one state *or* the other. Mastery would be the ability to sustain *either* state, one after the other.

Social influences are no less distracting than sense impressions. Deep social structures condition our goals and our ability to attain them, far more extensively than most imagine. Two notable examples are money and technology.

Money and everything that flows from it can become a lifelong distraction. Wealth, power, sensational people, places, and things—these appear to be worthy ends in themselves, requiring no justification. In an uncritical capitalist society, money appears to be a goal sufficient unto itself. Since money functions as a substitute for any and all material goals, it can easily become the ultimate distraction. Marx wrote of capital's "universal exchange value." Money is more seductive than any object, because it can be converted into any object. Thus money has come to represent any desirable object. Because of its power over things and people, it seems to offer unlimited possibilities for fulfillment.

However, once it has fulfilled every apparent need, rather than quieting desire money instead creates more needs than it can satisfy. It continuously promises "more" and "better", ensuring disappointment. It saddles its master with cares and anxieties requiring even more money, time, and attention to sustain. Even the very wealthy, who hire people to manage their possessions, are distracted by the concerns associated with those things. One concern is that those assets could become liabilities if their economic value diminishes; but a far greater threat is the liability possessions pose to their freedom. Money is often mistaken for freedom; but when one's possessions (not to mention the continuous demands of creditors, vendors, partners, employees, charities, solicitors, and family members for money) create these liabilities, hasn't the means subverted the ends? Hasn't the goal of freedom that wealth promises been undermined by money, the means to achieving it?

Consumer technologies offer inexhaustible opportunities for distraction. The unlimited potential for distraction represented by the "smart phone" is worthy of an entire field of study. Moving images and sound, continuously changing content, the power of social judgement delivered by social media, and the programmed compulsion of advertisements make the internet quicksand for the undisciplined mind lacking clear and compelling goals.

My first encounter with technology's unlimited potential for distraction was in grad school. I used a PC to write my papers, and back then Microsoft Windows was still a new operating system. Unlike its predecessor DOS, Windows let you work on several tasks simultaneously. In the early days of personal computing, the idea of "multitasking" was still promising. But I, for one, could never stay focused on the foreground screen. The "tasks" running in the background were always on my mind. Over time, I found that my main activity was switching from one task to another. The ends (the tasks) were absorbed by the means, the capacity and the mechanism of moving from one task to another.

I cannot explain why I needed a computer to write my thesis. In those days there were dedicated "word processor" machines. I could have bought one or borrowed one and gotten right to work. I also could have used a typewriter. Instead I wanted to build my own computer. I invested countless nights figuring out the obscure details of a system that vastly outstripped my needs (all I needed was a word processor). I was building a system that could have supported fifty "word processors" typing simultaneously. A system with ridiculous surplus capability—to support a goal that was not even underway. It needed to support just one writer—who wasn't writing, because he was too busy building the computer. Insufficient processing power was never a threat to my thesis. Distraction and lack of discipline was the threat. Here is another example of means subverting ends. The means to achieving the goal swallowed up the goal itself. Thus our most powerful tools, money and technology, can pose great threats to the goals that require them.

Chapter 12

A Pleasant Distraction

On Sunday nights I habitually took stock of my writing progress, and felt the weight of self-judgement most. This Sunday was no different. The noise of the TV, kids arguing, and persistent text alerts filled the background. Plagued with misgivings, I attempted to rally: *I must write tonight!* But there was just no way. So I pledged to myself, under threat of total condemnation, that I would write after work on Monday.

But on Monday afternoon I got a call from my old friend James, who was here in New York City for a couple of days. My friendship with James dates back to the year I spent in Chicago shortly after college. I hadn't seen him in at least ten years, and because of his reclusive instincts, he could easily disappear for that long again. Despite my self-loathing at neglecting my goal yet again, I really looked forward to seeing him.

We met at 7:00 at a steak house near Madison Square Park. When I meet an old friend, I'm often surprised by their age, because I remember them as a younger person. But James looked eerily the same. His secret was that he always looked old. When I met him in his twenties, he looked forty. Now in his fifties, he still looked forty. He was now (as I always remembered him) perfectly dressed, in a beautiful suit and overcoat, a white shirt and tasteful tie, and freshly shaved, as if he were on his way to a board meeting. This was always a point of pride for James. I was delighted to see that fussiness and punctilio were still very much a part of his character. He must have softened over the years, because he indulgently returned my hug.

Renewing our friendship over drinks and dinner, we reminisced about old times. Those old times consisted mainly of working together on the Chicago Mercantile Exchange in the late '80s. We could laugh about it now, but our bond at that time was one of mutual commiseration. We were runners—the peons of "the Merc". Our job was to run tickets into rowdy scrums of traders shoving and shouting at each other in the trading pits. The traders generally cursed or ignored us runners. Shit rolls downhill, and we were at the bottom. Like James, I felt completely out of place. But he really *looked* out of place—jarringly so. His shoes were always polished, his slacks always crisply pressed, his white, cotton shirt—never any other color—was starched and spotless. He dressed like an executive, but was, like me, just another peon. Some runners were kids right out of college who had some connection to the Merc (my dad worked at one of the brokerage firms with desks on the trading floor). Some were ballsy kids from the south side with just a high-school degree but knew a broker who could vouch for them until they proved themselves. Many of the runners were interested in a career there. For my part, I was there because my dad asked me to give it a try. He thought I'd like a career in finance and saw this as a valuable first step. I saw it as an awful place to work, but nevertheless interesting—in the way a general-admission heavy metal concert is interesting.

James was comically unsuited to the rough-and-tumble of the Merc. Nearly bald at twenty-six, he had a very imposing brow, which he wrinkled to great effect, showing every shade of surprise, concern, or disapproval. He smoked unfiltered Camels. James was gay, but rejected anything so effeminate as filtered cigarettes. Away from the Merc, his casual dress was that of a 1930s British bon vivant. He favored tailored suits with tapered waists and flared lapels. His shoes were far too expensive for his salary. He always wore hats, as if he were a film noir character—probably because of his baldness—but in fairness the Chicago winter is brutal to an exposed head. His go-to hat was the Stetson Saxon, with a soft, gray fur. He also liked the Fedora. It made him look hard, especially when smoking unfiltered Camels. Once James had the nerve to wear a Homburg to work. Brushed, black velvet with a tightly curved brim, the Homburg was indeed a perfect complement to his dark gray, pinstriped suit. Seeing him arrive at the Merc on any given day, one would have expected him to ascend the escalators to the executive suites, rather than descend to the trading pits.

James was not, as his style of dress hinted, the son of a rich British industrialist. He was born outside Hibbing Minnesota in 1956, into a poor, strict Catholic home, already inhabited by six brothers. According to James each brother, upon arrival, had been issued a color-coded set of towels and assigned a daily set of chores. Meals were as regimented as a mess-hall. His inexhaustible supply of stories from this barracks upbringing had me howling with laughter. This military uniformity extended from his home to the care of the Jesuit brothers in high school and college. James was destined for the seminary, but had deep doubts at the eleventh hour, and fled his family and Hibbing in shame. His expensive suits disguised his poor origins, making him the outward equal of the money men. But because of his pride and his fine education he distained the "mercantile" existence, though like everyone else, he needed a job.

Impeccable business style was James's way of declaring to the Merc's money men: *I don't care what you think!* Try to imagine the jeers his manner and appearance raised among the boors of the trading pits. Now imagine his reciprocal distain, as he held forth (privately) in high dudgeon—which, though artificial, was still impressive.

We were bored and above it all—at least, that's what our attitude was intended to convey. To get through the trading day, we traded ironies. We goofed on the people and the scene: packs of sweaty men, elbowing and jostling each other, shouting and arguing about the price of a piece of paper. Back in the '80s this method of trading (called open outcry) was still, in all its crudity, the mechanism of market liquidity.

My home base at the Merc was the S&P 500 Index and Options pits. Sometimes I was assigned to the Commodities pits, where my firm had another desk. James's trading desk was at the Currency pits. As far as I was concerned, he had it easy. Currency traders were far more civil than the brutish S&P and Commodities traders. James dealt with big shots by assuming a superior, "put upon" air, as one perpetually aggrieved by disorder, indecorousness, and poor taste. Somehow that worked for him.

Some of the runners were scruffy Chicago locals straight out of high school. The job was a great opportunity, because the next step up the job ladder was phone clerk. This job required no college education, just nerves of steel. The phone clerk was the "key man" at the trading desk. Man or woman, they were continually on the phone with the back office of the brokerage firm, and sometimes talked directly to big shots who traded from their private accounts. The phone clerk continually watched another clerk in the pit—the quote clerk—who quoted the market real-time with hand signals. Real-time manual quotes were more accurate than the numbers posted on the big board. With one phone in the crook of their neck, and another in their hand, the phone clerk would use their free hand to signal the pit clerk to buy or sell S&P 500 contracts.

The traders stood in a ring around the pit facing each other. The quote clerks stood back to back with their traders, facing outward toward the trading desks. They listened for the price of the last contract bought or sold, and quoted it continuously by hand signals to the phone clerks, who were sixty to seventy feet away but could not hear a thing due to all the shouting. Finally the phone clerk signaled the pit clerk to sell, say 50 S&P contracts for a price of 200. The quote clerk whispered the order into the trader's ear, the trader bellowed like a stuck bull, and the other traders jumped into action. When the order was filled, the quote clerk signaled the phone clerk then wrote down the trade on a trading card. The phone clerk then gave verbal confirmation to the client on the phone, and sent the runner to the pit to fetch the trading card and time-stamp it.

Phone clerks made better money than us peon runners. But if they were any good, they got the confidence and respect of the traders. That went a long way at the Merc. The reason was that in "fast market" conditions, it was easy to lose your composure. A lot of money was on the line. If you made mistakes, you didn't last long. In a fast market, when the prices reflected on the big board were way behind the real-time prices in the pit, traders had to trust the clerk implicitly. On their Reuters terminals, traders in the back office might see the bid/offer as 199/200, the same price reflected on the big board above the pits. But the pit clerk was quoting the last sale at a price of 196 and dropping fast.

Amid the panic and shouting, holding two phones, placing orders and time-stamping trading cards, the phone clerk had to maintain composure. If they were very good and got the backing of a powerful trader, they might get even get a seat on the exchange. This was an opportunity to make life-changing money. I knew of several traders on the floor got seats that way. With pluck and hustle and brains they had lifted themselves out of poor South Side neighborhoods to attain real wealth.

Under routine market conditions, the scene was just a bunch of middle-aged guys milling around, boasting, and telling bad jokes. Our phone clerk would write orders on trading cards, and with a flick of the wrist, time-stamp it and hand it to me. I'd run it out to the pit and hand it to the pit clerk or directly to the trader. When the order was filled, if no runners available, the quote clerk would throw the card back to the phone clerk—maybe sixty feet away—with amazing accuracy. The card was rectangular, longer than it was wide. Their technique was to bend the card, touching the top and bottom of the card together a few times until it was curved. Then, palm up, holding one corner of the card close to the body, the clerk would fling it, with a snap of the wrist. It rotated around an imaginary cylinder as it flew to the phone clerk, who, even working two phones, caught and immediately time-stamped it. I once saw our quote clerk Angelo throw a card from the pit directly into a phone clerk's jacket pocket.

Those time-stamped cards were watched very closely, otherwise there would be hell to pay the next morning when we did "the breaks". Every morning, we got a stack of cards recording each trade that was made the day before. We compared them with a printout of yesterday's trades from the back office. If a trade was missing, or if it didn't match up with the price, we had to wander around the pits before the market opened to find the broker (often hung over) who had taken the opposite side of the trade, and determine what the price really was.

As I ran my peon rounds, I periodically bumped into James on the trading floor. We exchanged ironic barbs, about how the two of us, atheist and believer, served side by side "at the altar of Mammon". About what new injury or insult we had just received from a certain trader or clerk. About what limited human types are found at the Merc. About how pointless the whole system was. Irony was our *lingua franca*. We were thrilled with our cleverness and convinced of our superiority. He used phrases like "the altar of Mammon" not because of his Jesuit education but because he was an insufferable elitist. One day shortly after we met, as we passed each other during our rounds, James handed me a note on a trading card:

"inter oves locum praesta, et ab hoedis me sequestra"

I recognized this from the Latin mass. "Place me in your flock (Lord), and keep me from the goats." By goats was meant "tainted horde".

So the next time I saw him I stuck a trading card in his pocket with this message:

"Statuens in parte dextra".

This was the next line of the liturgical verse: "Seat me at your right hand." Now I wonder, all these years later, if he took that as a come-on. Anyway, after that we were inseparable at the Merc.

It was late when we finished our last bourbon. Looking around, the steakhouse was empty now, and the waiters were clumping together, looking at us expectantly and ready to close up. I walked with James for a few blocks to find him a taxi. As a yellow cab stood by, I seized him in a robust man-hug. Even a little drunk, James was too stiff to embrace me for long. Still I held on, marveling that at this late hour, after much steak and whisky, his tie and collar were still perfectly arranged, and there was still a faint scent of lavender, masculine and tasteful, lingering about his overcoat and scarf. I knew James well enough to understand I might not see him for another ten years—if, indeed, ever again.

That is the mixed blessing of living in New York City, that *axis mundi,* the center of the world. People continually come and go. I could have dinner with interesting people every night if I wanted to. But living here is like living in the information booth at Grand Central Station—distraction doesn't stop until you deliberately pull down the shade. There's never enough time to do everything you want, or to see everyone you want. I thrive on the feeling that I *could* do anything at any time, if I wanted to—that constant sense of unlimited possibility, right at my doorstep, that makes New York City so exciting.

And yet, how often do I take advantage of these unlimited possibilities? Why do I persistently feel I should be doing more? Why do I feel a twinge of regret even after a memorable evening with an old friend? *How perfect today might have been, if only I had not neglected my goal!*

Oh, human perversity! Must we always seek satisfaction elsewhere?

Chapter 13

Procrastination

Would I be able to write today? By sheer force of will I now stood before my writing chair, fearing the lacerating self-doubt that lay ahead. Through the window behind my chair I watched the sun sink slowly into a luminous nest of orange and purple clouds as they flattened and spread across the western horizon. I had to turn my back on this beauty. I had to turn inward, face my fear, and get started.

I set my laptop on the coffee table. The glare on the screen showed greasy fingerprints and dust. I found some Windex to wipe down the screen, and this action suggests I clean the glass coffee table too. But I must first clear its accumulated junk: a mug half-filled with morning coffee...an empty water glass...books and magazines...pens...cat hair...the top of a Häagen-Dazs pint. This step suggests I pick up my kids' wayward clothes. After that, I find myself standing, unaccountably, in front of the open refrigerator. Behind the appearance of meaningful action, a terrified, paralyzed creature crouches in the darkness, witnessing his compulsive, automated behavior, and unable to break it. In these desperate moments, barely keeping my head above the churning whitewater of procrastination, I did not have the presence of mind to write the next chapter. But I could, at least, write about my immediate struggle—in other words, about procrastination itself.

I. Minor Procrastination

Forcing myself into my writing chair, I examined the turmoil of my mind. All procrastination seems to begin with a given objective or obligation. It's usually a small thing: "I'm going to the gym after work." Procrastination challenges that assertion with a simple counter-assertion: "Maybe tomorrow…." In this simple way, procrastination divides the commitment into "now" and "later." It doesn't negate the claim, but compromises it by pushing it off into the future. It defers the obligation by temporizing.

Procrastination is alluring because it presents an additional "choice" where one did not exist before. I did not say I *won't* go to the gym; I said I won't go *today.* I haven't really shirked my obligation, I've just delayed its fulfillment. Procrastination offers an alternative to yes or no, to the either/or of acting or failing to act. Procrastination offers a third way.

Mark Twain famously quipped: "Why do today what you can put off until tomorrow?" This is often how we deal with minor duties that are unpleasant to perform. Examining my own behavior, minor procrastination looked like simple pain-avoidance. We cast our obligation off into the future—perhaps with the hope that it never return.

II. Major Procrastination

But pain-avoidance does not explain all procrastination. For we also procrastinate about commitments that are pleasurable. This suggests deeper forces at work. For example, a friend has invited me to see his band play at a certain bar on any given

Thursday night. I knew I would enjoy it, if only I could get there, but I procrastinated about it for months.

Another example: I'd been invited to meditate with a friend at his temple any Saturday morning. I am interested in Buddhism; I really wanted to go (I told myself) but I put it off again and again. I compulsively deferred the question. I kicked the can down the road. This can't be explained as simple pain avoidance, since I did want to go.

What these two examples have in common is not aversion to pain but aversion to *change*. There is an outward and inward component. We often dodge commitments that require a change in our schedule, in our comfortable routine. Procrastination functions to maintain *status quo*. The reinforcement of our routine hides a deeper aversion: uncertainty, or fear of the unknown. For a long time, we may believe our "reasons" for procrastinating. But if we acknowledge in our hearts that we still want to keep our promise, then these excuses ring hollow. Why would we continually put off something important to our happiness?

(i) Rationalist

Major procrastination may wear the mask of rationality. It can coopt reason into examining an intention comparatively, or "in perspective". Comparison immediately creates doubt about whether our intention deserves the highest priority—which in turn allows justifications for inaction to arise.

One form of rationalist procrastination is the persistent demand for "more information" before committing to action. This objection cannot in principle be overcome. It is always better—in principle—to have more information. But since information is forever incomplete, action may be forever delayed.

For a critical fact might arrive at the last minute and "change everything".

For a student writing a thesis, this rationale wears a scientific mask. Before she can start writing, she must first read the primary sources. Then she must read the secondary sources; then the commentary; then the commentary on the commentary. The student believes she is getting incrementally closer to valid judgment—but this is an illusion. High anxiety accompanies every attempt to make an "objective" judgment. Procrastination uses the "need more info" fallacy to indefinitely delay decisions.

Procrastination helps to subvert conviction. I claim, *"I will write at six-thirty"*; but as six-thirty approaches, procrastination parses that imperative into several alternatives: "I'll just feed the dog and make a cup of tea, and then I'll write." Procrastination places our inner imperative side by side with other possible actions, thereby equivocating its value. Procrastination is a "leveling" process[10] that converts a claim of absolute value into something of merely relative value. It reduces our value-claim to the point where it is "just as good" as any other. This kind of procrastination could also be called skeptical. For it reduces *qualitative* difference (in which one object is superior to another) to *quantitative* difference (in which objects differ only in degree): "Since I can't write now, I'll write later"—as if these two things were the same.

Practical reason is infatuated by options, and will defer or delay commitment to entertain them. Options are typically "one of many"–type choices that encourage procrastination. In moral terms options are non-choices because they require no sacrifice and engender no commitment. Seeking alternatives for every decision is surely perversity. Indeed, the mere *thought* of limiting risk (hedging) may be sufficient to undermine commitment.

(ii) Escapist

Major procrastination appears to have an escapist element—a regressive desire to shirk one's obligations, e.g., the external demands made upon us by work, family and society in general. We are continuously under the dual spotlights of social judgment and self-judgment. Escapist procrastination expresses a desire for relief from the demands of "the universal"—our conscious and unconscious accountability to norms. Our desire to withdraw from the spotlight of social judgement is a *yearning for indeterminacy.* This yearning is a daydream in which we are freed of obligations.

The demands of "the universal" are unconditional. But life, by contrast, is fluid, changing, and conditional. The role of the goal seeker is, in general, to make his conditional life conform to the universal, in this case, the Great Goal. But the chemistry of procrastination works against goals, dissolving the bonds of commitment back into their more fundamental fluid and conditional state. Escapist procrastination lifts the crushing weight of norms, obligations, and commitments from the seeker's sagging shoulders—if only for a moment.

III. Existential Procrastination

The burden of freedom—choice and action—is a basic condition of human existence. Day in and day out, we must choose and act, choose and act. The burden is heavy; every choice demands sacrifice and has consequences. The burden of freedom is crushing. It never stops; there is no rest or refuge. Our only hope is to forget. This is the function of existential procrastination. If minor procrastination is the evasion of pain, and major procrastination is the evasion of change, existential procrastination is the evasion of death. Existential procrastination enshrouds us in the illusion of a durable life, obscuring our final end. It keeps us rooted in everyday life, keeps our back to the destabilizing feelings of insignificance, mortality, fear and uncertainty that death implies.

I remembered Janáček's words: "Our Great Goal reminds us that we must act now—and that we have limited time. It reminds us of our fundamental limitations, and so—indirectly—of death. It draws death out of the shadows of anxiety, helping us to clarify the end and through this clarity, what we *must* do before we die." The Great Goal gives death a form that we can grapple with and directly act upon.[11]

IV. The Symbolism of Necessity

Helpless, rudderless, storm-tossed on a sea of doubt, waves of distraction crash over my head. I am the doomed sailor in Poe's tale of terror, *A Descent into the Maelstrom.* The maelstrom is a freak of nature, a gigantic whirlpool that forms near a remote Norwegian island as the tides change. It swallows anything that comes within its orbit, reducing great ships to matchsticks, crushing their hulls with inconceivable violence on the rocky sea floor. When the tide turns again, the maelstrom slows and flattens, and the pulverized wreckage rises to the ocean surface.

The narrator of Poe's story is an experienced sailor who has fished these remote waters with his brother for many years. But one day they miscalculate the tides and their ship is caught by the maelstrom. They try every conceivable tactic, they exhaust their skills, but they cannot not break free from its titanic force. Giant seas, fierce winds, and total darkness make sailing impossible. They are drawn ever closer. As their ship lurches over the lip of the giant funnel, the brothers brace for death. But instead of toppling to their destruction, the ship lurches downward briefly, then settles into a rapid circuit along the vortex wall.

Witnessing this fearsome spectacle of nature's power and awaiting imminent death, the narrator's terror is replaced by awe, and in this moment of calm reflection he notices that some of the debris rotating around the funnel descend more quickly than others. Suddenly it occurs to him: there is a way!

Through horizontal rain and waves crashing over the ship, he sees his older brother across the deck, holding on to a bolt for his life. He signals to him with wild gestures. He shouts himself hoarse: *Abandon ship!* But he can't make himself heard over the hellish roar. With his brother watching in horror, he lashes himself to a wooden barrel and leaps overboard.

Half-expecting immediate death in the violent churn, instead he found—after several circuits of the great funnel—that he and his barrel were descending more slowly than the ship. The ship, he could see, was sliding faster down the vortex wall. With each circuit they separated further.

Finally the ship, with his brother clinging desperately to the deck, tumbled into the monstrous howling maw. Now he counted the minutes to his own death. But soon the maelstrom began to slow. The funnel gradually flattened, and debris began to rise up to the surface. His bold action had saved him from destruction.

The *maelstrom* is not unlike distraction and procrastination–implacable natural forces that can overwhelm human freedom. They are only different in scale. The seeker struggles against these forces, desperate to chart his own course.

He refuses to be absorbed by nature. In the jaws of death, he asserts his freedom in a wild gambit. At tremendous risk he leaps into the void…and behold, he is free!

Chapter 14

Inner Life

In one bold act, I had defeated those powerful forces of nature, distraction and procrastination—in my imagination. This daydream expressed nothing so much as the impotence of my will, and my failure to make any headway with my book. Months ago, I had set sail on the dark seas the Great Goal. Every day I face fierce headwinds, I am nearly driven back to where I started. Each day I begin and am defeated anew.

Every sentence was shot through with uncertainty. Every inch of progress was a strenuously self-conscious act of will, measured, weighed, doubted and dismissed. Why was it such a labor, what was wrong? Why couldn't I ignore these doubts and write freely? I felt a powerful desire and could muster willpower on demand, but it wasn't enough. What I needed was commitment. Commitment must be rooted on unshakeable ground, anchored by beliefs unseen by the light of reason because they are more ancient and predate it.

For many weeks I idled at this impasse, helpless, chafing with frustration and uncertainty. Then one night I fell asleep in my writing chair and dreamed I was digging. I watched my hands dig along the base of a great stone wall, immeasurably long and high. They finally stopped at one spot to dig deeper.

I thought: Commitment is near! If only I can reach the other side!

I watched my hands, with broken nails and filthy skin scraped raw, frantically digging down. Finally they reached softer earth and found a hollow at the base of the wall. They uncovered a gap between the massive foundation stones. As I drew closer, I felt a moist breeze, like a breath against my face. The hair on my neck stood up. On the other side of this wall, I knew, were the sacred grounds of commitment! My heart surged with conviction.

After squeezing through the gap I was completely enveloped by a humid darkness. But as my eyes adjusted I saw that it was not completely dark. The outlines of a strange subterranean landscape gradually came to light. It seemed I was overlooking a great cavern. Its roof was supported by soaring pillars of rock, each dimly lighted by different hues; or perhaps they glowed from within. Apart from these great columns, everything was in deep shadow, and I feared getting lost, or falling into some rocky crevasse. I groped forward blindly, with shuffling steps or on all fours, and finally reached the floor of the cavern. Emerging from the shadows I reached the first pillar, which glowed with a faint bluish light. As I approached, I somehow grasped that it was one of the core human values, absolutely fundamental to human meaning.

Now I felt a distinct, uplifting feeling—a sense of great possibility. This pillar, I felt, was the *sense of freedom.* As I stood before it, an inner voice gave me to understand the following:

*

"The sense of freedom is a fixed feature of inner life. The feeling that we can act at any moment, if we so choose, is universally presumed.[12] Even if we are physically restrained or disabled we say to ourselves, "If I wasn't restrained, I would certainly act." We sense that we are always free to try. This intuition of our freedom is seen in our unquestioned conviction that we can do little things at any time, like turn our head, or flip a light switch, or make coffee. We equate this sense of spontaneity with freedom.

Our natural conviction in the freedom of our actions is also seen in the responsibility we take for them, for example in feelings of regret. If we thought our actions were not free—in other words, if we knew that we could not have acted differently—we could not feel regret.[13] We'd know without a doubt that events had to occur the way they did. It is the thought that we could have acted differently that produces regret.[14] This thought is based on a deep presumption of freedom.

However, just as we cannot choose what our next thought will be, we can't predict the will's action a moment from now, much less tomorrow. The will has its own dynamic and like thought, it is both spontaneous and unreliable. If we say, "tomorrow I will go running," this signifies only that we are willing now to go running tomorrow. But tomorrow we may no longer be willing. It would be more accurate to say, "I will go running tomorrow, if I am willing." As we all know from experience, that is a big *if.* It might happen, and it might not. We cannot control whether and when the will wills. Our actions are conditioned by the willingness of the will, which we cannot control. In this strict sense, we can never be free.

But even if the sense of freedom is just an illusion, it nevertheless *feels* like freedom; and perhaps that is sufficient. For the sense of freedom is needed to provide meaning and direction in an uncertain world. And even if freedom is only an idea, it is an idea with greater causal power in history than all of Caesar's and Napoleon's armies."

The oracle of the pillar, that voice I heard from within, suddenly ceased and I felt an urgent need to find the next pillar of human value. No sooner was I engulfed in darkness, than the pillar appeared just ahead, glowing dimly in alternating reds and oranges muted but warm and welcoming, and rising to the very vault of the cave. This pillar was unmistakably the *sense of empathy*. Inwardly, I was given to understand the following:

*

"The sense of empathy is the ability to intuit another person's inner life. Not to *know*, but rather to sense that there is another inner life opposite one's own. Empathy makes it possible to see in someone's suffering not a thing but a person. The power of empathy varies greatly among humans.

There is the story of the traveler who was robbed, beaten and left for dead by thieves on the highway. One rider and then another saw a mortally injured man on the side of the road but passed him by. They could see it was a man in distress, or dead. But feelings of fear or uncertainty or inconvenience drove them past. But the third traveler to come along was different. He felt the same concerns as the others, but empathy overcame those fears. He identified with the victim's suffering as his own, and acted with compassion. He nursed the man's injuries and saved his life. Empathy is the seedbed of the two great social virtues, compassion and love."

*

There seemed to be a path connecting the pillars of human value, for I made my way quickly to the next column, which glowed with a white – though muted – light. Approaching the third pillar I felt a sudden surge of benevolence to all things, and in addition a sense of rectitude, a deep conviction I was on the right path. This pillar, I readily grasped, was the *sense of goodness*. I stood rapt before it. For its existence has long been questioned by scientists and philosophers, and now it was revealed to me as the truth: there is an innate sense of goodness in humans.

Inwardly, I heard the following: "The sense of goodness is the ability to recognize that things are qualitatively different, i.e., some are better than others.

It is natural to believe that goodness is a quality inherent in things themselves. The most comprehensive expression of this view was offered by the great medieval theologian Thomas Aquinas. The cosmos and all that it contains is good, because it emanates from the greatest good (*summum bonum*), or God. The world is good because God is good. Everything, including human beings and human souls, incline toward the good just because they incline toward God.

Five hundred years later, the philosopher Emmanuel Kant got much closer to the truth when he found that the good had a subjective, inner ground. Goodness is not based on objective qualities, nor does it emanate from God. Rather it is based on an innate human capacity Kant named "the fact of reason". The fact of reason allows humans to grasp and conform to a universal criterion of goodness called the "categorical imperative". This criterion states that we should act in a way that we would accept as a universal rule for all others, including ourselves. The fact of reason guides us to do the right thing—but not by necessity. It leads us to the good, but cannot make us choose it. We are free as moral agents to acknowledge the fact of reason and conform to it or accept responsibility for resisting it. Even though inclination to the good is built into the structure of the human psyche, we are still free to choose or to reject it."

Thus spoke the oracle of the pillar of goodness.

*

I moved on, trying hard to absorb this last lesson, and soon found myself standing before the next pillar, which glowed dimly with multiple colors, alternating and interacting with each other. I stood entranced, captivated by this vision, until I grasped that this pillar represented *the sense of beauty.* Listening inwardly, I heard the following:

"Beauty is not a quality of certain objects. Nor is it found in any particular object. Rather it is an inner state felt when the understanding and imagination enter into dynamic interaction or "free play". Beauty is not in things, but in the inner eye of the beholder. [15]

The sense of beauty is not necessarily felt in the presence of a rare landscape, a perfect sunset, or even a world-renowned work of art. It is not as rare as any of these things. Often, it arises under very mundane circumstances. A cloud of steam, a dead tree branch, a surprising shape, a bowl of fruit, broken glass—seemingly arbitrary images and experiences can spontaneously produce the sense of beauty. The reason is that it is not the object, but the inner experience—the play of the faculties—that produces it.

The sense of beauty does not directly produce motives, intentions, or action. It suspends judgement rather than advancing it. For the sense of beauty is not a means to an end, but an end in itself. It has intrinsic, not extrinsic value.

But can't beauty be highly motivating? Didn't Helen's face launch a thousand ships? If beauty is not an object or its qualities, but just the subjective play of mental powers, how can it produce action? How could beauty "move" the beholder? The answer is, when this inner state is regarded as—mistaken for—an object of interest, beauty may activate the will and the desire to "acquire" the beautiful object. The will requires an object to act upon. Once beauty is misapprehended as an object, it falls into the domain of the will.

An example is found in the famous poem "Archaic Torso of Apollo," in which the image of human perfection the poet sees in the statue of the god makes him yearn for a higher state. It reminds him of his goal. In the midst of a spiritual crisis, beholding the statue, he hears inwardly a thundering imperative:

You must change your life![16]

This imperative arises not from thought, but from the unconscious. Its truth is not rational, but visceral. It announces a calling of the poet to account, revealing a great disparity between him and his ideal. This aesthetic imperative, highlighting the gap between the self and the good, is authoritative, and is followed immediately by the seeker's deep yearning to close this gap. In this conviction the seeker feels the "healing Apollonian power" and is moved to meaningful action."[17]

*

Suffused now with conviction and energy, I moved quickly to the next pillar of stone, which, much brighter than the others, was easy to find. My eyes rose from the dark base of the column, which rose from the cavern floor to the vaulted ceiling, where colorful veins of rock branched out, extending to the all the other columns, linking them in some kind of mineral communication. Standing before this unique phenomenon, I felt a powerful sense of connection between all things, and, not least, between the pillars of value themselves.

"The *sense of connection* must not be confused with the *idea* of connection. From the idea of connection we might deduce the multiple and various connections between things. But the sense of connection is not an idea, it is an *intuition* of the fundamental relatedness of all things. There is no individual meaning or thing, distinct from its connection to all other things. The notion of an inherent, atomic meaning is a natural illusion caused by the structure and limits of the senses and brain. The sense of connection includes all creatures, making possible a common humanity. In its absence—when the sense of connection fails—we unfailingly regard ourselves as isolated individuals who can act privately, without any consequence to others. But just as there are no isolated things, there are no "isolated" acts. Indeed, the meaning of individuality itself is defined by social and historical context."

*

I shuffled along for a while in near darkness, when finally, by chance, I stumbled upon a vast dark column. It had no light source from without or within. Looking up I could see that, unlike the others, this column was not distinct from the cavern wall but embedded in it. It rose like a great tree from the cavern floor and branched into the darkest recesses of the surrounding walls and ceiling, tapering off into total blackness in every direction. I sensed a presence that enfolded all of the cavern, the entire earth, indeed all of existence. I felt a *sense of the absolute,* immediately followed by a sense of my own insignificance.

"The *sense of the absolute* is rarely felt in daily life, and it could easily be overlooked when it is felt, as an oddity or aberration. It is an intuition of all reality and its deepest ground, all that it contains, and all that lies behind it. The absolute is all that is; it is Alpha and Omega, beginning and end, the source and purpose of the universe. It is 'that which cannot be contained by anything else'. These attributes of the absolute are not deduced by logic, but felt, often with a sense of awe or dread. The sense of the absolute can be overwhelming when it occurs, and may make an individual feel vanishingly small. It can produce deep emotions and life-changing experiences.

The sense of the absolute is often interpreted as the presence of an absolute sentient being, or God. When understood in this way, faith, receiving commands from God, produces action. The power of faith is based on the belief of the faithful that their actions must conform to God's law—in other words, that their actions are *necessary.* For the faithful, this necessity is extremely motivating. Faith is in this sense the very paradigm of subjective necessity. It produces in the faithful the conviction to act. Faith can indeed accomplish great things, some of them seemingly miraculous. Moreover faith is not seriously challenged by rational arguments or conflicting evidence.

Does the nonbeliever lack the sense of the absolute? Absolutely not, since it is a fundamental human intuition.

Rather, the sense of the absolute is reflected into conscious awareness in two different ways. For the believer, it is reflected into consciousness as an absolute being. For the non-believer, the intuition is reflected into consciousness as absolute space. For the believer, this intuition is more likely to produce action; for the non-believer, it is more likely to produce contemplation."

*

One pillar remained. To reach it required steep climbing up the far canyon wall. Atop that wall was a pillar that seemed to support the highest and broadest vaults of the cavern. Climbing higher and higher I asked myself, is this the way out of the darkness of inner life? When I finally stood before it, it became clear what had driven me: the *sense of purpose.*

"The sense of purpose is a feeling that we act for a reason, that we are driven by an end. Ends or purposes are readily seen in nature. The purpose of an acorn is a mature oak tree; the purpose of a baby is to become an adult, to reach its mature form. This is the meaning of the Greek word *telos*—the outward purposiveness of things. But humans also have a *telos* of inner nature (the subject) which consists of deliberately chosen actions and goals. It is not sufficient for humans to just pursue their natural purposes; they want to choose their own purposes. An innate sense of purpose, combined with the ability to learn and improve, is the basis for continuous human development."

*

I had visited the seven pillars of value, and now I just wanted to get out of the cave. I couldn't find a way further up the canyon wall, so I had to climb back down again. Soon I became lost in a dark and treacherous region. The path narrowed and dropped off on both sides into blackness. Without the pillars to guide me, I was terrified to move. I crawled and groped my way blindly forward, trembling with fear.

Gradually my breathing slowed, and I heard a rushing sound. Too frightened to stand, I crawled toward it. I came to a swift black stream. Utterly lost, with no hope of retracing my path, I waded fearfully into the stream and let it carry me downstream. Whether it would deliver me from the cave or fling me into some abyss seemed equally likely. A faint glow appeared on the horizon and gradually brightened, like the eastern sky just before sunrise, and I now could see the rocky ceiling and the shoreline of the river. I was borne along by Lethe, the stream of forgetfulness, out of the cavern of inner life. Where Lethe flows from underground and meets the upper world, it turns into a stream with a different name: the Stream of Busyness.

Chapter 15

Busyness

I woke to a rushing sound, my face pressed against the bulkhead of the plane. Brilliant light poured in from the oval window in front of me. I heard a flight attendant recite the landing script: "Ladies and gentlemen, as we begin our descent into L-A-X International Airport, please make sure your seat backs and tray tables are in their fully upright position. Please ensure your seat belt is securely fastened and all carry-on luggage is stowed underneath the seat in front of you or in the overhead bins. Thank you."

I righted myself, grabbed my carry-on, and shuffled into LAX terminal, stunned by the light and activity. I caught the shuttle to the Hertz rental lot, rented whatever they had (a blue Nissan Altima)—and drove directly into a traffic jam. I was surprised, once again, by the misery of driving in L.A. Very unlike the misery of driving in New York—but that's a separate topic.

The traffic was interminable, but polite. Coming to a dead stop on the freeway, I answered a text from my daughter, and an email from the client I was visiting tomorrow. Forty-five minutes later, I pulled up to my hotel. Blocking the valet parking area was a vintage red Mercedes convertible. A tall, bald man sporting a long beard and dark sunglasses was leaning on the car. Perhaps sensing my annoyance, he stalked toward me with long strides, then pulled off his glasses and smiled.

"Mitch!"—I leapt out and greeted him with a hug.

"Let's drop off your stuff," Mitch said, "I have plans."

"Plans! I've been on the road all day" I whined. "What I really need is a drink. How about we head up to the rooftop bar?"

"Alright" said Mitch, "maybe just one".

The last time I saw him, about two years earlier, he was smooth-shaven and had long black hair (with a few strands of gray), which he usually tied back in a ponytail. With the bald head and beard, and his impenetrable black shades, he looked like a freak. I said "Mitch, you look like a freak." He seemed to enjoy that.

Mitch is a former New Yorker who made a lot of money in commercial real estate, working in his third-generation family business. And he could have made a lot more, had he followed the family script. But he grew tired of New York, and he always wanted to collect and restore cars. I'd swear he moved to California for the cars. He had nothing keeping him in New York—if he ignored his mother's anguished arguments. Tall and handsome, at age forty-two he was a confirmed bachelor.

When he lived in Manhattan, he was a solid, grounding presence for me. Someone I could talk to about serious things, but, equally, someone I could talk to about nothing. When he told me he was moving to L.A., I made no pretense that he should go and pursue his dreams. For my own selfish reasons, I told him he'd be crazy to leave New York.

"Dude, you're a man of depth, a man of substance. How can you live in La La land? What are your chances of meeting someone like you out there? Plus, you hate blondes...."

"No, my mother hates blondes" he objected.

"And you hate fake boobs" I parried.

"No, *you* hate fake boobs."

I sighed in disbelief. "C'mon Mitch, think it through. LA is a cultural wasteland. How can a man of your taste and discernment feel at home there?" Here I was simply flattering him, and he did not disagree. "What about your family, what about your long-suffering mother? What about your people?"

"News flash, chief. A few of my people do live in L.A. For example, my uncle and his family. So big deal, for the High Holidays I fly back and make Mom happy."

Before I finished my twenty-dollar drink, Mitch declared we're going to another place, Perch, a favorite of his.

"But really, why? I'm perfectly happy right here."

"No, we gotta go." Mitch says. "No worries, it's close."

Outside, the valet pulls up with Mitch's car, a fire engine-red Mercedes-Benz 190 SL Cabriolet Convertible, circa 1961. This work of art is a complete answer to my loose talk about taste and discernment. Once Mitch is behind the wheel and we are out on the road, I understand. He just wanted to get out and drive his car. A beautiful night, a great friend, a fabulous car. To me this is self-explanatory. Mitch always had forceful arguments for enjoying life. As if on cue, with a big smile on his face, he lit a fat-cat cigar. We drove west (away from the restaurant, but it didn't matter) to enjoy the beautiful sunset. I'm not a car man or a cigar man, but I get the appeal.

Finally we had dinner, but because of the time difference, I was useless for conversation by eleven o'clock. On the drive home, though, I wondered aloud. Life can be so fucking hard in New York. What was the point of all that effort? Was I straining to the utmost under the illusion that satisfaction lay just ahead? One day, but not today, I'll take a break. One day, but not today, I'll reward myself. One day, but not today, I'll enjoy myself, I'll take stock, I'll tie loose ends, I'll give back, I'll be happy. What if that story is an illusion? Maybe Mitch had figured it out. He knew how to work hard, but he was no masochist. He enjoyed himself without contradiction or guilt. I had a lot to learn from Mitch.

The next day was surprisingly easy. My meetings were painless, and by three o'clock I was at Venice Beach having drinks with another old friend, Melissa, an L.A. native who came to New York in the '90s and returned ten years later. She lived in Cobble Hill in those days. She had that rare quality of intense personal focus. Her undivided attention (so rare in the modern world) made you feel valued and important. Amid the constant distractions of phones and computers and social media, few things felt better. In this I had something profound to learn from Melissa: not just the power of focus, but the power of focusing on people.

How satisfying life can be, when you have no other goal than to enjoy the company of a good friend! How satisfying when you relax and concentrate on the details. How captivating, how enchanting life can be! One moment flows seamlessly into the next, with no time for reflection, no time for doubt. Despite the recent fires and floods in the hills around L.A., my two good friends seemed truly calm and relaxed. They knew how to enjoy life. I needed help with that.

On my return flight, descending into LaGuardia, I received a calendar alert on my phone.

MAYA'S WEDDING, Saturday May 12.

I totally forgot! I would be home only one day, before I had to drive to Washington for a niece's wedding. From there, Diane and the kids would drive back, and I would fly to Orlando for a conference. Thursday I would return to two furious days of catch-up; then Saturday I had to visit my mom in New Jersey.

I was fully re-absorbed into life. I hadn't had time to myself in weeks. But it no longer mattered. I no longer thought of my book, and there was no question of writing. It was simply not happening. My "new normal" was pure status quo. I was happy, or so it seemed, just to keep up with life.

Just as paving stones are overgrown by grass, my fixed time slot for writing (6:30-8:00 PM weekdays) was reclaimed by my calendar. I gave it up without a fight. I would not miss the daily doses of lacerating self-doubt. I would not miss those unhealthy feelings—the persistent sense of uncertainty, of incompleteness, of a permanently unfulfilled obligation. For so long, the Great Goal had hung over my head like a sword. Why continue abusing myself like that? Why prolong the pain?

The hounds of the Great Goal—that tracked me remorselessly, barking and baying when I strayed from my commitment — the hounds of the Great Goal were in retreat. I could hear their yapping, tapering off in the distance. To evade them, to throw off the scent, I waded into the the swift Stream of Busyness, that enchanting state of preoccupation and perpetual activity where the hounds could not follow. I am borne along in full and pleasant forgetfulness of the Great Goal for weeks, then months. I find satisfaction every day now, in daily challenges, in friends and family, in lightness and laughter, in every kind of enjoyment, great and small. I find meaning in trifles again. I have rejoined the human race. I go to the gym, or meet a friend for a drink, or meet my wife for a movie. I walk my dog, chat with neighbors, go to dinner, watch TV with my kids. I reclaim those casual, carefree moments the Great Goal had stolen from me.

Busyness is a term Kierkegaard used to satirize the compulsively active *hommes d'affaires* of his time. The Busy are forever dashing here and there, meeting important people, making introductions, making deals, flattering some and pressuring others. They are fully absorbed into day-to-day existence.[18] Their business and personal lives are all-consuming and leave no time for reflection. They are convinced of the importance of their schedule and believe their most sacred duty is to manage it. For the busy, a full and frequently double-booked calendar is a badge of honor. For it leaves them with no free time to question the reason for all their busyness.

Because it meets with social approval, busyness can become a way of life—a life of permanent distraction. As Kierkegaard wrote: "...the general approval is everywhere upon the side of the busy one—everywhere, in the ever-increasing pressure of busyness, and in the swarming mass of excuses."[19]

The busy rush headlong from place to place, convinced of the importance of their time, without considering, for a moment, that something higher needs their attention, something greater than their income or social advancement. In perpetual self-absorption, the busy avoid the question of the true purpose of their lives. For the question of one's real purpose is a doubtful one, a fearful one. Thus doubts and fears are put off, deferred to another time, and cast back into the onrushing Stream of Busyness.

But one day the busy, in a rare moment of solitude and reflection, grasp that busyness does not lead to happiness.

When the busy come to doubt where busyness leads, they seem to have three options: (1) Vanquish busyness and focus on one great thing: that goal which is *necessary* for them—and embrace, with the goal, the sacrifice it demands; (2) abandon their goal in a deliberate and considered fashion. After weighing the pros and cons, they resume their former, safe path, and put a good career, an enjoyable life, and comfortable retirement ahead of their Great Goal (generally speaking, a prudent thing to do); or (3) neither choose *nor* abandon the great goal, but instead press unreflectively forward, and continue avoiding the question. Maintain *status quo.* This is the most common path. Distraction, procrastination, and busyness continue to hold sway. Busyness provides a permanent refuge from the truly important. Busyness offers an escape from the Great Goal.

This default choice—this non-choice—was my path. I avoided the question. And yet I could hear in the far distance, if I listened closely, the hounds of the Great Goal, yapping in pursuit. My master was hunting me again, and I was in full flight.

*

THE PARABLE OF JONAH AND IRA

There was no mistaking God's plan for Jonah. It would radically change his life, and he was afraid. He knew he was not equal to the challenge—to preach God's word to unruly barbarians in a foreign land. He was devout, but he was desperate to escape the awful burden of God's mission. He tried to run. He thought he could avoid God's all-seeing eye.

Jonah lingered in the back alleys of Jaffa, near the waterfront, waiting for night to fall. *Incognito,* he sought a ship to take him abroad, to some far off land where he could hide from God. Stepping out of the shadows, eyes darting like a criminal's, he approached a skipper on the pier. Sensing Jonah's desperation, the captain demanded a usurious price. But Jonah was too terrified to object. He paid his passage and took his berth. Trembling beneath the deck, he thought: *I can escape this awful fate! I will be invisible among the masses. Not even God will find me .*

We know from the story that the ship soon sailed into a violent gale. The captain, a devout man, understood that this violence was God's anger, and they would all perish. At the height of the storm's fury, the captain found Jonah asleep in his berth. He suspected Jonah had offended God, who would take retribution on them all. A sacrifice was needed to appease Him. In the midst of chaos, they drew straws; Jonah drew the short one. The terrified crew cast Jonah into the sea. He struggled for a while on the rough waves; then the unbelieving crew watched, aghast, as a black monster rose from the sea and swallowed Jonah whole.

Immediately the seas calmed and the skies cleared. The ship sailed without incident to Tarshish. Beneath the waves, however, a different story unfolded. After swallowing Jonah, the Leviathan dove to unfathomable depths—to the foundations of the Earth. For three days Jonah lay in the belly of the beast, trembling in a black pit of dread and remorse. In his darkest moment, in deepest despair, Jonah finally repented with all his heart. He repented his evasions. He begged for another chance to show his faith, to take up God's plan again. He gave himself to God. Immediately the Leviathan bore Jonah to the shore and vomited him up. Jonah wasted no time.

He prostrated himself on the sand, offered thanks and praise to God, and, with undivided heart and mind, walked straight to Ninevah to fulfill his mission.

A conventional way to read this story is that Jonah was God's instrument. There was no avoiding God's plan. Jonah ran, and sailed abroad, and was thrown into the raging sea, but still could not dodge his fate. The whale snatched him up and delivered him to his mission.

But it can also be read as the story of a man who ran from his highest purpose. He saw the challenge of greatness laid before him. But he was afraid. He feared the sacrifice, he feared giving up his former life, his former self. He fled the *burden of change* that greatness had thrust upon him. Who among us are like Jonah—hiding in fear from the greatness we know lies within?

There is another, apocryphal, story of Jonah that presents an entirely different question. In this version of the story, Jonah had a brother named Ira, and they were inseparable companions. So much so, that God called upon them *both* to preach at Ninevah. They were both sorely afraid, and together they ran from God. They crept onto the ship that night, keeping to their berths. But when the gale reached a divine fury, Ira (in mortal fear) whispered to the mate that Jonah had defied God. The captain and terrified crew cast Jonah into the sea. Ira watched Jonah struggle on the waves—and then, to his horror, he saw a black monster rise from the depths and swallow Jonah whole.

Immediately the seas calmed, the skies cleared, and the ship sailed without incident to Tarshish. Ira felt an awful remorse, but, even more than that, he felt fear. Would God find him? He found lodgings in an obscure quarter of the city. He kept his head down; he went by another name. At length he settled in, and gradually, his fear subsided. He found work, he married, he assumed a normal, quiet, invisible life. He could not believe his luck! God, inscrutably, had let him go.

Like Jonah, Ira fled his destiny. But unlike Jonah, he succeeded. Ira's story is that of a *potentially* great man, who procrastinated and dodged, who hid from his highest purpose—and succeeded. Ira, having dodged his trial of greatness, sought the slumber of routine existence. He sank into the narcosis of daily life, of comfort and routine. Hiding from his highest purpose, Ira remained permanently *incognito.*

But Ira never found tranquility in his refuge. He felt God's eye continuously upon him. The price he paid for the comfort of an untroubled life was the constant awareness that he missed his chance for greatness. For the rest of his life, Ira was like a slumbering night watchman, who awakens with a jerk whenever he remembers his duty. But he is watchful for only a moment before the ticking clock lulls him back to sleep again.

Chapter 16

The God Of The Great Goal

Finally raising my head above the frothing Stream of Busyness, I heard a booming voice: *Come back! Return to your goal at once!* I was in full flight now. I had fallen out of favor with the God of the Great Goal. But I no longer found solace in busyness. The enchanting forgetfulness of constant movement, novelty, variety, spontaneity, pleasure— the joy of full, heedless immersion in life—was gradually denied me. The painful awareness of my commitment had broken the spell of busyness.

I had wandered away from the citadel of commitment, I had lost myself in busyness, and now desperately sought to return. But now the moat bridge was drawn and the portcullis closed. I was banished from the Kingdom of the Great Goal. I might never muster the commitment to re-renter again. I turned away to wander in a strange barren country, a no-man's land between duty and neglect. I languished in a purgatory, neither hot nor cold. I was an exile from both lands, from the beauty of forgetting, and the rigor of remembering my goal. I drifted aimlessly in a permanent twilight of recrimination.

However virtuously I might act—no matter how steady in my habits, dutiful as a son, supportive as a father, loved as a husband, constant as a friend—still, a sense of unfulfilled duty stole the pleasure from everything. It was a constant background irritation, like gastritis. Even joyful occasions fell under the shadow of the neglected goal. I found myself thinking, *What a great day this would have been, if only I had been true to my goal.* The Great Goal eclipses the meaning of everything, leaving the beauty and value of daily existence in permanent shadow.

The God of the Great Goal is a jealous god. He demands the sacrifice of all other goals on the altar of the Great Goal. Eventually, every meaning, every value, derives only from its relation to the Great Goal. It plunders the value of each and every little thing, to feed the one great thing. The kingdom of the Great Goal is an inverted world in which its absolute value, rather than anchoring and enhancing the meaning of lesser things, instead bleeds them of meaning. The Great Goal provides a unitary and unquestioned source of meaning, but only at the expense of the rest of reality.

The God of the Great Goal giveth; the God of the Great Goal taketh away. He offers greatness, but only at the expense of satisfaction today. He promises the future, at the cost of the present. He promises a kingdom of heaven, but only at the cost of happiness on earth.

Chapter 17

Country Idyll

My behavior was driving my wife crazy. She knew I needed to finish the book. She could see I was getting nowhere, and my anxiety was mounting. I'd sit for hours, day after day, making no progress. I ignored everything around me, adding to her workload. She might sit down and tell me a story from her day. I would peer over my laptop screen and try to look engaged. But I couldn't close the laptop; eventually, my eye would drift back to the blank screen. I understood this was atrocious behavior. But I was drawn` irresistibly back into the vortex of the empty page, where no one could save me. Drastic measures were needed.

I had so many excuses for why I couldn't write. I had tried various rituals, incantations, and other implausible techniques to ensure that I wrote every day. I had tried everything but physically removing myself from the scene. So I began driving upstate on the weekends, to Sullivan County where I had an old farmhouse. Built in 1850, it stood on a rugged plot of land with woods and boulders, hills and fields, and a little catfish pond. Maybe quiet and solitude was what I needed get this monkey off my back.

Diane was very receptive to the change. I was no longer pleasant to be with. Even when we were out together I was permanently distracted. Her expectations of me at home were generous—there were none. She did not demand attention. She expected very little. And yet I sank below even these expectations. Crushed by the burden of the book (so my justification went) I fell well short of social utility.

Sophia and Jane were teenagers now; their weekend plans no longer involved us. That left my dog and cat, Juno and Bruno, for companions. Bruno was a big gray cat who found his way into our shed upstate. He spent the winter there, insinuating his way into the house in the spring. The girls immediately adopted him, as if stray cats had well-established asylum claims. We brought him back to the city, but he loved coming back. So on many a Friday night, the three of us settled into the minivan for the two-hour drive to the house.

I thrilled to the prospect of great unbroken tracts of time for writing. I loved arriving at night, stepping from the car into the moist dark air, into the rhythmic chirping of the tree frogs. The sky, bedazzled with stars, descended to the rooftop; one could sense here the true dimensions of the cosmos. Exhaling deeply, I felt a visceral relief in returning to the heart of nature.

By the removal of many things (so went my logic) I could focus on one thing. I could no longer plead distraction. By drastically reducing outward activity, I could focus on inward activity. This was my chance to grapple, once and for all, with my Great Goal. A final accounting was needed. Either I finish it or it finishes me.

The maximum I could write was four hours a day, if I was lucky. So the remainder of the time I could spend on home projects, which in an old house are innumerable and continuous. This would be therapeutic, I was sure. Finite tasks with a beginning and end. Success at small projects is satisfying and salutary for a weakened will. And I would in turn apply the workmanlike attitude I take toward home repairs, to my writing.

In an apartment of course, the most onerous homeowner responsibilities fall to the super. But in an old house, repairs continually cry out for attention. There is no end to them, and no super to fix them.

Sitting in front of my laptop, I thought about the insulation falling from the basement rafters. Winter was coming, and it had to be done soon. I also had to replace the leaky water heater, fix the gutters, repair the broken step on the deck, replace the third floor toilet—and so on *ad infinitum*. Each task called out me. They might consume a year of weekends, if I never wrote a word.

One Saturday morning, I woke early as I always do, and went downstairs to make coffee. I found my laptop and prepared to write. As the water heated in the kettle, I looked out the window and saw that a bear had knocked down the bird feeder (again). I put on my boots and took the aluminum pole holding up the feeder (which the bear had effortlessly bent in half) to the shed, straightened it with a vise, then carried it, with a sledgehammer, a length of rebar and a stepladder back into the yard. I pounded a new hole in the ground with the rebar, inserted the aluminum pole, and placed the feeder on top. I headed for the shed to fetch the bird seed, but heard the kettle screaming—I had forgotten the coffee. I bring my coffee outside, then remember the birdseed, put my coffee cup down, fetch the seed and carry it to the feeder, climb the ladder, pour the seed, gather the tools, go back to the shed, then finally sit down to cold coffee. Just then I notice the layers of fallen leaves under the maple tree. With winter coming, they had to be raked up. Twenty minutes later I had a pile of wet leaves. Normally, I cart them down the hill to deposit on a great burn pile. But last winter two rosebushes died from the cold, so I'll use the leaves to cover the rosebushes. First I prune the roses down to short stalks. Then I dump the leaves and spread them around, cover the roots, tamp them down. Finally, I go inside to make breakfast, stopping at the bathroom to wash my hands. I find the toilet tank is not filling properly—the feeder valve must not be working, so I turn off the feeder valve. I'll have to drive to Home Depot to get the part—after I write, of course. I head upstairs to the second floor bathroom and notice that the windowsill is full of dead ladybugs, which every year find a way into the attic and die *en masse* there. Some crawl through walls, attempting to escape via windowsills, but to no avail. That's life in the country. Having plugged every visible hole in the attic, I still can't stop the ladybugs from returning each year. I open the screen and sweep the ladybugs out the window, but then notice that behind the radiator there are scores more, dead. So I go to the bathroom closet, get a broom and dustpan, and sweep them up. But before I throw the dead insects away, I go upstairs to check for ladybugs on the third floor. Every window casing is full of them: hard little red pills with black spots. I remove the screens and sweep them out. Then I check the attic spaces, under the eaves of the roof, and see piles of them, but it's too dark to clean them up. So I go down to the first floor for a flashlight but find the battery dead. With mounting hysteria, I go down to the basement, find another flashlight, carry it to the third floor, and peer into the attic. Thousands of ladybugs, little red pills, are waiting to be swept up. I turn off the flashlight and notice a tiny sliver of light coming into the attic from outside. *Aha! That's where they get in!* I just need some insulation to stuff into that hole. But the insulation is in the basement. So I head down there again, three flights, but I forget I need gloves so I don't get fiberglass fibers in my hands—so I head to the shed to find gloves, then back to the basement, get a piece of insulation, then tramp up three flights of stairs, and plug the hole in the attic wall.

Now I'm ready to put aside this trivial bullshit and focus on my sole purpose, my one thing: writing. I head downstairs with the best intentions but notice that clods of mud had fallen from my boot treads onto the third-floor staircase. I sweep these up, but it's mud, which smears, so I head downstairs again to the kitchen to get the all-purpose "green" cleaner and wipe up the mud. Closing the door to the third-floor stairwell, which has a large window, I notice how dirty the glass is. I spray some all-purpose "green" cleaner and wipe the glass but it dries all streaked and foggy. Then I realize, of course, you don't wipe glass with "green" cleaner, you use Windex. So I go back downstairs to get Windex in the pantry closet under the stairs but it's not there. I always keep some in the car, so I go out the front door of the house to find the Windex. Which I do, and then, grabbing more paper towels, I go upstairs to clean the glass.

By this time, mounting the stairs yet again, my anxiety has reached a boiling point. I look at my watch—10:47. I was supposed to start writing two hours ago! I am suddenly stricken by the thought that all my actions are meaningless, compulsive, utterly determined. I am an automaton controlled by the forces of distraction and procrastination. I know what I should do, but I am a captive of my body, and I must do its bidding. I am in a panicked, if mechanical, flight from my goal.

Maybe if I was a more mature writer, or had more discipline, or just had a better idea for a book, these tasks would not be so distracting to me. I might have the self-control to devote the morning to writing, and the afternoon to projects. But I had none of these things. Instead, in my upstate refuge, I had become a host-body for procrastination. I watched as, with each home repair, I systematically evaded my goal. I did exactly the opposite of what I knew I had to do. These activities might be enjoyable in their own right—if only they were my intended actions. Instead, they were so many vehicles of my destruction, so many pathways to madness. Existential procrastination had returned with a vengeance.

Chapter 18

Somnambulism

Such was the bliss of my upstate refuge. Wherever I looked, I saw projects that might consume the rest of my life. Moldings, floors, radiators, paint, curtains, weather stripping, insulation, gutters. Everything needed repair or replacement. My refuge had turned into a labor camp.

One afternoon in late October, I was in the basement, hanging insulation, when I saw something odd. The foundation of the house had been laid in 1850 with big slabs of bluestone, rocks and mortar. On top of the foundation lay the original rough-cut beams on which the house stood. Protruding from the base of a foundation wall was a ceramic pipe from which a continuous stream of fresh water flowed. The regular flow of water carved a winding path through the dirt floor of the basement, flowing downhill to the lowest point, and exiting beneath the foundation through another ceramic pipe, so the stream could run through it. Years ago I was advised by the house's previous owner—do not try to seal up the basement. It had been that way for a very long time, he said; don't mess with it.

Later additions to the house did not have full basements beneath them, only crawlspaces, to give access to pipes and insulation. To provide better access to the crawlspace, one of the builders had removed some big stones from the top of an interior wall, near the boiler. I was stapling insulation to the rafters when something caught my eye. Within the blackness of the crawlspace maybe fifty or sixty feet away, I saw a thin shaft of light. It revealed in its narrow beam a tiny wisp steam or smoke. *What is that? Water vapor? Weird,* I thought. *Makes no sense. There shouldn't be any water there.*

I did not want to go into the crawlspace. It was very dark and night was falling. My neighborhood plumber was always away this time of year, visiting his grandkids in Florida, so he couldn't look at this any time soon. Winter falls fast up here, and if it's a leaky pipe, I might have to fix it before he returns. I grabbed my oversized industrial flashlight and focused its beam to extend its reach. Now, where the wisp of smoke was, sat Bruno—motionless, tall and regal like those cats adorning Egyptian tombs. As I moved the flashlight to him he disappeared into the blackness. Just at that moment I remembered I was trying to master procrastination. So I went back to hanging insulation and forgot about it.

In my forties I began to experience insomnia, and needed Ambien to sleep. At least in the city I did. In the country, I could sometimes fall sleep without it. On Ambien, I remembered no dreams. But when I stopped using it, vivid dreams reappeared. My sleep became reanimated. I was a sleepwalker when I was a kid. So, when I woke up one night in the living room, standing in front of the basement door, it did not strike me as odd. I returned to bed and thought nothing of it.

As a kid, my sleep was never quite sound. My mother said that when she checked on me before going to bed, she sometimes found me sitting up, eyes wide open, talking in my sleep, something she found "eerie." Many times I had woken up, on my feet, in different rooms of the house. I woke up once in the back room of the basement in total darkness, standing in front of my dad's workbench, and found my hands fumbling with the tools on the pegboard. Once I awakened in the front room of the basement, behind the fabric my mother had hung like tapestry in front of the cinder block walls. To this day I remember that dream: I was trying to rescue someone who was buried behind the walls. That particular dream was scary, and finding myself behind a curtain, feeling my way along a cold cement wall in the darkness of the basement was bizarre. But I was no longer alarmed to wake up in such circumstances.

The same thing happened the following weekend. I woke up around three o'clock in the morning standing in front of the basement door, this time with my hand on the doorknob. This did not concern me as a child; still less did it concern me now.

Then, one Sunday morning, I woke up and walked to the bathroom to pee. Passing the mirror on the way to the toilet I stopped dead. I was stunned—staring back at me was a wild animal. I was naked, and my face and chest were smeared with dry mud. My stomach and thighs were red and scratched. My fingernails were black with dirt. I stood there, dumbfounded by my own image. I immediately ran downstairs to try the basement door. It was unlocked.

I threw the old mechanical light switch at the top of the basement stairs and stepped slowly down the rough planks. I didn't know what I was looking for. As I got closer to the boiler, what I saw gripped my heart with fear. The opening to the crawlspace— the top of the stone wall—was smeared with mud, the same mud that scraped off my body as it exited the crawlspace last night. Instantly, I was seized by a hair-raising feeling of exposure and vulnerability. Standing naked in the dirt basement, covered with mud, trying to think clearly—I had the inexplicable sensation I was being watched.

Slowly, uncertainly, I retraced my steps to the second floor bathroom and took a shower. I made coffee and ate breakfast in a daze. After a while I calmed down and moved seamlessly into my self-made labyrinth of procrastination. As I was sweeping the kitchen floor, I suddenly remembered that I had seen something strange in the crawlspace a few weeks before. Had I been trying to investigate this in my dream?

I put on an old Polartec jacket, leather gloves, and a wool cap, found a flashlight and went down to the basement. Standing before the crawlspace, I reached up and grabbed one of the floor braces, got my knee on the gap in the wall, and pulled myself in. I shimmied toward the front of the house in a military crawl. What I found there was...mud. But it shouldn't be wet there. I pointed the flashlight at the rafters, found the hot water pipe, and spotted a right-angle joint, dripping. Did this explain the mist I had seen a few weeks ago? It was a good enough explanation for me. I started backing out of the crawlspace on my elbows when my flashlight passed over a pile of rocks, just behind the front porch, and I saw beneath it a patch of darkness so black it caught my eye. *What is that?* I changed direction and crawled forward again for a closer look.

It might have been a raccoon or possum or skunk den. I did not want to get caught in a crawlspace with a rabid animal—or any animal, for that matter. I searched for a stick, but all I found were rocks, so I threw them into the blackness. They disappeared, one by one, without a sound. I shimmied up close enough to shine my light directly in... then felt a warm, moist breath on my cheek. A chill ran down my spine. Starting back in alarm, the ground just in front of me crumbled and fell in. I grabbed one of the floor braces above me to support my weight, then pointing the light into the hole I saw a gradual rocky drop-off, going down maybe fifteen or twenty feet.

What the hell? I thought. *A buried oil tank...an old septic tank? A cave? What* is *this?* It made no sense. I quickly reverse-crawled down the crawlspace, back the way I had come. As I backed out of the gap in the basement wall, I felt my stomach scrape against the rocks. Now standing, I felt a powerful *déjà vu,* and again felt I was being watched. I had the very strange impression that I was an actor in a horror film, unaware of my fate. *Bizarre.*

I could no longer trust my senses or my mind. Was I cracking under the strain of hysterical procrastination? Was I panicking at the imminent threat of failure? Dizzy and disoriented, I tramped robotically up the basement stairs, lay down on the couch in the front room, and fell immediately into a deep sleep.

Chapter 19

A Dream

I found myself standing in an audience, in a stone amphitheater, watching a tragic play. The hero was just about to fall on his sword. By his willfulness and pride, he had betrayed his city, destroyed his family and dishonored his name. He had lost every reason to live. But before taking his life, he had to explain his flaws and the forces that had driven him to this fate, in an overlong soliloquy.

Suddenly, with a fanfare of horns, and a flash of light, a god approaches! It is the Genius of Equivocation. Well known to the audience, this spirit can resolve any contradiction. The Genius uses whatever means are at hand to dispel differences: association, assimilation, suppression, denial. No matter what the conflict, he is able, with apt phrases and convincing arguments, to make it disappear. He is a true *deus ex machina,* appearing at just the right time to rescue the hero from his existential bind.

Genius of Equivocation (to Hero, genially): Do not be concerned about failure. It is transient, my friend, it will pass. Like everything in nature, it

> must change. Failure is but a moment in the life of the ever-evolving self. Failure is not the end, but a transitional phase of development. It should not be the cause of such anxiety and grief. The great inner turmoil of human striving, from doubt to conviction and back again—is all unnecessary suffering. For failure is merely a mental construct, a state that does not in fact exist.

But the tragic hero, familiar with dialectics, shakes his head angrily.

> **Hero (angrily):** The essence of failure is *finality*, not transition. When an enterprise fails, it is over. Failure is not a means but an *end*—a terminus. A terminus is not a process of change, but the opposite. Your version of failure involves no suffering, no accountability, no finality, no loss. It is the opposite of failure, as I know and feel it. [20]

But the Genius has a ready answer:

> **Genius of Equivocation:** Unless one's failure coincides with one's death, it must turn into something else. Change is the unchanging law of the universe. Life will continue; failure will ultimately be folded into your experience. For it is not truly loss, just a path to a different goal. It is not an end but a means, not a terminus but a transition. Failure points to the future.

The hero replies:

> **Hero:** I have lost everything. This is the *end* of my effort, not the beginning. Maybe a god can't understand frail humanity. Loss is the very heart of mortality. It is permanent. It cannot be reduced to a logical term. Do not disparage failure by dressing it up with platitudes, presenting it as something agreeable. Failure proper is categorical. It is not figuratively—but actually—the end. But enough of dialectics.

He draws his sword.

The Genius stays his hand.

> **Genius of Equivocation:** This is just a misunderstanding, young man. A simple error. Loss is not final or permanent. Loss, negation, non-being—it is not a black void into which precious things fall. Negation is a truth interwoven into everything, at every level of existence. Your notion of loss, young man, is dialectically incorrect. Your painful feelings are understandable, because you are mortal. But this deep sense of loss will, over time, be woven into the fabric of your life.

In parting, the Genius blesses the Hero with a gold coin bearing his wisdom in an inscription: 'Non ausi, nihil perdidit'. *Nothing ventured, nothing lost.*

Chapter 20

Forest Interlude

I woke from the dream pinned to the couch, my eyes fixed to the ceiling. I couldn't move. Every intention, every interest, every purpose had left me. I could not see what to do next, what to think next, what to feel next. I could not justify the least movement, the slightest action. At that moment, I could not have found a motive to scratch an itch. Doubt had infected the very heart of my will.

In my soul the two necessities, inner and outer, were locked in mortal combat. I was host to the world's Great Battle. In the heat of this battle freedom was mortally wounded. Outer necessity had the advantage; with one decisive blow, freedom would perish. Where could freedom find refuge?

In this desperate state I remember Septimus, the traumatized war veteran in Virginia Woolf's story *Mrs. Dalloway.* Septimus thought:

> The whole world was clamouring: Kill yourself, kill yourself, for our sakes. But why should he kill himself for their sakes? Food was pleasant; the sun hot; and this killing oneself, how does one set

> about it, with a table knife, uglily, with floods of blood—by sucking a gas pipe? He was too weak; he could scarcely raise his hand. Besides, now that he was quite alone, condemned, deserted, as those who are about to die are alone, there was a luxury in it, an isolation full of sublimity; a freedom which the attached can never know.[21]

Like Septimus, I lay helpless,

> ...a relic straying on the edge of the world, an outcast, who gazed back at the inhabited regions, who lay, like a drowned sailor, on the shore of the world.[22]

Just then movement caught my eye—a tree branch, swaying outside the window.

Suddenly the sky darkened, the wind howled. Juno sensed the change, ran to the door and scratch at it mechanically. Finally my legs swung to the floor, and I moved, unthinking, to the door. Juno threw herself against it, tearing the doorknob out of my hand, pushing the door wide, and dashing into the yard as if her life depended on it. She looked back at me as she ran with what looked like a grin, her tongue flapping from her mouth like a flag. The commotion startled two does foraging under an apple tree near the woods. One doe stood stock-still, but the other raised her white tail like a flag and bounced away. Juno gave hot chase.

The second doe followed the first, falling in closely behind, and became Juno's target. With explosive speed and ferocity Juno lunged at the doe's haunches, trying to take a bite. The gamey perfume filling her wet nostrils awakened the coldblooded killer lurking beneath the cute puppy exterior. The doe, wild-eyed and desperate, ran for her life, and, in two great leaps, was over the stream. Juno, mad with bloodlust, bounded after the doe with renewed vigor.

The property abuts a thousand acres of state land. I ran after Juno, but, a few seconds second later, she was out of sight. I started to walk, calling her periodically. I could still hear the thumping of hooves and thrashing of leaves as Juno tore through the woods.

Suddenly, a gust of wind with fine ice crystals brushed my face. Steel gray clouds rushed in. The sky darkened two shades. The sun became a low, pale, silvery orb. A snow devil appeared overhead then was instantly borne away into the upper air. A steady snow began to fall.

"JUNO, COME!"

I'd spent a lot of time in these woods. I knew walking west would get me home—or at least get me to the road. But now, scanning the horizon three hundred and sixty degrees, I could no longer see the setting sun. The woods are uniform in winter: myriad dark vertical poles against a white background in every direction. Juno might find her way back with no problem, but I might be left wandering in the forest all night. I would have to head back soon.

"JUNO, COME!"

I walked and listened, walked and listened. I heard only a low moaning wind, creaking trees, and the periodic mad calls of wild turkeys. Without bearings, was I just going deeper and deeper into the woods?

Ahead I saw a clearing, and as I got closer, a delightful surprise—a fawn, curled up against a fallen log. I crept up, not yet knowing what I saw. The faun lay motionless. Its features emerged slowly out of the gloom.Its big dark eyes, its delicacy and helplessness stirred in me a powerful sense of compassion. Charmed by the encounter, I squatted down and watched for a moment. The mother, probably sensing danger from Juno, left her baby there and could not be far. So I moved on, tramping toward the clearing, bright with freshly fallen snow.

Stepping into the field, I felt a shock: a dark shape, a large animal stood motionless on the opposite side, just inside the woods. The forest had gone silent. My heart pounded in my ears. *A hunter?* Indeed it was hunting season. *But who hunts at night?* Frozen in place, I caught my breath and waited for the creature to move.

At that moment moonlight broke through the cloud cover, bathing the clearing in an eerie blue glow. From the dark forest background there emerged an elongated face, suspended like a mask in the moonlight. Above the forehead, deeply etched with lines of hardship and experience, stood upturned ears or horns. The mask recalled the ancient forest god Silenus.

Inwardly, I heard the voice of the satyr: *Like nature I am immortal. But you, fleeting humanity, live only a day. Death is ever present. Why squander your short time in the bounty of nature with strife and worry? With all your cares, it would be better if you had never been born! Abandon all ambition! Surrender to delight and wonder, to music and song, to wine and ecstasy. Surrender to the earth!*

As surely as I stood there motionless, my sneakered feet frozen in the snow, I was vouchsafed the eternal wisdom of the forest god.

Suddenly I heard a great commotion in the forest. Now Juno burst into the clearing and rushed at the dark shape on the other side. But the face withdrew instantly from the moonlight and disappeared silently into the woods, leaving Juno standing perplexed in the snowy glade.

"JUNO, STAY!"

She remained riveted there as I stepped into the clearing, took off my belt and looped it through her collar as a leash. Turning my back to the rising moon, I knew I was facing west, and we set off through the woods for home.

Chapter 21

Spelunking

I woke up again that night in front of the basement door. This time I found my hand not on the doorknob, but fumbling with the key. An ancient skeleton key was always in the lock and was quite hard to turn. Concentrating, I turned the key and when I heard the bolt, it was immediately clear what to do—I had to go into the cave.

The sky was already brightening; there was little point in going back to bed. I made some coffee and breakfast, got dressed, and went outside to the shed. There I found two nylon ropes, a multi-tool, two flashlights, a bubble-pack of D cell batteries, and gloves. I went back inside the house, found a backpack, candles, and matches. From the kitchen I grabbed two bottles of water, two apples, and a box of granola bars.

I went down to the basement, climbed into the crawl-space, and crawled military style toward the front of the house. I looked up and saw Bruno again, sitting serenely in the same spot, and as soon as I saw him, he disappeared into the hole. "Bruno!" I called. *Great,* I thought, *now I have no choice. I have to go in.* I tied the rope around the floor braces, and lowered myself down a bit. The dark cavity before me was not a buried tank that had rusted away, but a much bigger space. It was not a vertical drop, but sloped. I let out rope as I let myself down, seat first. At the bottom, I found myself in a chamber—maybe ten feet by fifteen feet in size; the floor and ceiling were very uneven, so it was hard to tell. I looked at my watch: 10:20 AM.

Clambering around at the bottom, I found the chamber roughly torus-shaped, like a doughnut, solid in the center and hollow around it. But the doughnut only went perhaps three-quarters of the way around. I did not see Bruno. Crouching, I crab-walked around the doughnut, to where the floor sloped up sharply, and found a gap of eighteen inches or so between the top of the wall and the "ceiling." Kind of like a big mail-slot. I crawled up the slope on my hands and knees and looked over the top of the wall. I saw total blackness... then felt a warm moist breath on my face. My neck-hairs stood on end. *Another cave!*

I was easily able to climb through the gap. On the other side, instead of a steep drop, I again found a slope downward, this time more gradual. I tied the second length of rope to the first with a secure knot, and lowered myself down.

It seems I had entered near the ceiling of a sizeable cavern. I could not discern much detail because of the limited range of the flashlight. I looked out from my perch. The chamber looked quite large, maybe a couple of hundred feet across. The slope before me was like a saddle, dropping off evenly to my left and to my right. It looked as though I could easily descend on either side so I chose the left.

I was seized again with a sense of wonder and disbelief: *A cave under my house? Impossible!* But I pinched myself—and I passed the pinch test. I was soberly aware of where I was and what I was doing. Indeed, it occurred to me that I should not go any further without telling somebody. I felt I should probably go back. But I decided I would just go down the rope, have a quick look, then come back up.

The "floor" of the chamber where I touched down was roughly horizontal. I could stand comfortably. The ceiling here was maybe fifteen feet high, though lower in other places. Columns of rock (stalagmites?) rose from the center of the floor, but making out their shapes was difficult. To the left I found the cavern wall. I then turned right and slowly made my way along it. Keeping the wall to my left, and following its contours, I periodically looked to my right, toward the center of the chamber, using the rock columns as my reference point.

I wanted to see if light was still visible from the top chamber where I had come in, so I turned off the flashlight. The onrushing blackness compressed my heart like a vice and seized me with a profound dread. I switched the light on again, and the panic immediately passed.

Turning the light toward the center of the cave, I saw gaps between rock columns, and through these gaps I could see what appeared to be a wall on the far side of the cavern. It might be possible to climb through those columns to the other side, I thought. But for my own comfort, and to maintain my orientation, I would follow the perimeter of the cavern, keeping to the left. I continued along like this for fifteen or twenty minutes until a big rock formation along the wall blocked my progress, and I had to go around it. It was very slow going, as I had to creep along on all fours while holding the flashlight. I came to a relatively flat mass of rock, sat down, and ate a granola bar.

It was all so...*weird*. I turned the flashlight toward the ceiling and saw something remarkable—what seemed to be veins of ore, in different colors, overlapping each other. I made a mental note about the location, because I wanted to come back for a closer look. Maybe this was an illusion, created, somehow, by the flashlight? Then, as if to test this, I turned off the flashlight. Again the total darkness flattened me, like a crushing blow. My sense of self instantly shrank to a point of light, floating on a shoreless black sea. The absolute blackness, so rarely experienced, was terrifying. I switched on the flashlight...and everything was fine again. I checked my watch: 11:50. I had already been down here longer than I planned. Still, the way back was very clear to me.

I ate an apple and another granola bar, drank some water, threw the wrapper and water bottle into the backpack then started off, working my way around the chamber. It appeared to be roughly oval or football-shaped. I had entered at one end of the football, and then for more than an hour worked my way along the wall almost to the opposite point. I would just continue following the contours of the wall until I had made my way around the entire chamber.

Chapter 22

Failure

I made good progress for another twenty minutes or so before I realized I hadn't looked toward the center of the cavern for a long time. When I turned the flashlight in that direction I heard a gasp escape my throat. Instead of a view across the cavern, I was facing solid rock, just a few feet from me. I was no longer on the perimeter of a large cavern, but inside a corridor or tunnel. But this was impossible. I had stuck closely to the left wall. Had I somehow veered left and entered another chamber? I was dumbfounded. I heard my heart pounding in my ears.

I would just go back the way I came. Turning around, I stuck close to the right wall, the wall that had been on my left as I entered this chamber. I moved along this way for some time, thinking I would soon be back in the cavern. I kept peeking ahead with my flashlight, expecting the ceiling to open up into the main chamber. But it did not. Instead the tunnel became gradually narrower. I couldn't make any sense of it. The wall of the tunnel should have been curving to the left, toward the great chamber; instead, it curved very gradually to the right, as far ahead as I could see with the flashlight. But this was impossible, because as I entered this chamber from the cavern, the wall on my left, curved to the right. Was I completely turned around?

Suddenly, I panicked. A violent spasm of fear shook my body from its very core to the hairs on my skin. The possibility of getting lost had never occurred to me. I felt a sudden wave of vertigo, combining sheer incredulity with terror. My legs were wobbly, so I sat down where I stood. How did I get here? I would not take another step until I sorted this out. The great chamber had to be close. Somehow, I had taken not one but two wrong turns off of it. Now I realized I could die here. Whatever choice I made, I had to be sure.

To save battery life, I took a candle from the backpack. I had a dozen or so tea candles and a couple of stubs of table candles, four or five inches long. I lit one of these stubs, let some melted wax drip onto a rock, set the stub into it. I put the other stub in my pocket, and tried to think things through. In candlelight, the tunnel looked very different. Impenetrable blackness pressed in from both directions. In one direction was life; in the other, death; but which was which? Either direction was terrifying. No sooner did I favor one way, then I thought of why it was wrong, and why the other way must be be right. I went through this tortured calculus, back and forth for many minutes. I felt the weight of the rock above me, the weight of the world, slowly crushing me.

I checked my watch: 12:45. I had to go back the way I had come. This time I would always stay to the left side of the tunnel, thinking it would go left toward the big cavern. But before I had gone twenty feet, I saw that the tunnel curved to the right as far as I could see, and that I had no choice but to reverse direction again. In a panic, I lunged forward in the darkness and hit my head full stop on a rock. Everything went black and I had a dream.

I dreamed I was in a gloomy woods, crouching behind a tree. I heard the sounds of someone approaching, and I saw a prince from an ancient time clad in battle gear, stalking purposefully past. He stopped before a tree with brilliant yellow leaves, then, raising his sword, struck off a branch. He made his way quickly through the woods, through darkening hills and hollows, until he came to a sacred grove guarded by an old priestess, waiting impatiently for him. The prince raised the branch proudly; the priestess scowled. She had assigned him this task only hours before, and was surprised he returned so quickly. Without the "golden bough", the sybil warned, the prince could not descend into Tartarus and find his father. Without it, the sibyl warned, his descent would be pure madness. Now, she grumbled, she had to make good on her promise to lead him to the underworld.

The sybil led him across a dark, denuded landscape, vapors rising around them, to the mouth of a vast cave. There was very little light, and it was unclear how to proceed. Then the sibyl, in sepulchral tones, gave the prince this final warning:

Facilis descensus Averno; noctes atque dies
ianua atri Ditis patet; sed revocare
gradum evadereque ad superas aras,
hoc est opus, hic labor [23]

I woke up to find myself stretched out, face down, breathing hard. The flashlight was on. I rolled over and saw I was lying in a very narrow tunnel, too small to sit up in. I was in a totally different place! I checked my watch: 3:35. More than two hours had passed! Somehow, unconscious, I had gone deeper into the labyrinth. How did I get here? How far had I come? Now I had no bearings whatsoever.

I felt something crawling on my cheek, and I grabbed at it; I looked at my glove and found it wet with blood. My forehead had a large bump; I was bleeding from a gash.

Just then I realized—my backpack was gone! And with it—batteries, food, and water. Without it, I would die. An awful death, of hunger, thirst, and exposure. Without light there was no hope of escape. I switched off the flashlight to save batteries and gather my thoughts. The void rushed in. I concentrated desperately to keep shreds of myself from flying away into its vacuum. All I could think of was the mountain of rock pressing down. My heart pounded in my chest, filling my head and the tomb around me. I turned the flashlight on again, put it under my chin, and crawled crablike, feet first, down the tunnel in the direction I must have come. After about twenty feet, the tunnel let out into a small chamber which opened to the right.

No backpack.

I sat down and began to grasp the absurdity of my situation. I found myself in an impossible predicament. My body had, of its own accord, taken me to this place. It was impossible to know what direction to take. *One way leads to life, the other to death. Or both lead to life—or both to death.* It was Russian roulette. I had no choice: I had to choose.

I turned off the flashlight and saw something odd—what looked like a faint spot of light, some distance away. Was it was an afterimage from the flashlight, still lingering on my eye? I turned my head to the left...the light disappeared, all was blackness. I turned my head to the right, and it reappeared.

What the hell?

I pointed the flashlight to the right and turned it on. I was looking directly into the tunnel I had just come out of. I turned off the light again. Now in fact, some distance down that narrow tunnel there appeared to be a very dim light, or, rather, a small patch of shadow, but not utter blackness. I crawled toward the light, tearing my knees and palms on the rocks in the desperate hope it was the way out. But as I moved toward it, the light did not seem to get any closer. I lay my head down to rest, and then a few minutes later opened my eyes, to find total darkness in every direction. Had it just been a cruel illusion? I looked at my watch's illuminated dial: it was 4:35. Had sunlight somehow filtered down from above? Had that spot of light winked out with the last rays of the sun? That seemed just possible. How else could it be explained? Whatever the answer, this tenuous hope was the final thread connecting me to life.

I laid my head down on my gloved hand. Knowing that night was falling calmed me somehow. Twilight is the prettiest time, up above. As the sun dips below the western hills, the sky turns by fine degrees from blue to pink to violet. Gradually, the birds go quiet, leaving only the occasional songs of the robin and blackbird. Past the pond, in the woods, the footfall of deer can be heard. I imagine I glance downhill, to where the field meets the woods, and see two does standing stock-still, sensing my eyes on them. Slowly, they return to their former business, foraging for food in the grass. The stars wink in from the east, one by one.

My dog and cat must be hungry by now—I didn't feed them this morning. What did they do all day? Are they looking for me? In my concern for them, I forget my plight. Now I thought of Diane. She never required check-ins from me. She never asked me about my plans, never questioned what I was doing or whom I was meeting—a great blessing for any man's dignity and composure. We hadn't spoken since Friday—and that was fine with her. But now I realized she might have called today. I closed my eyes, thought of her and my children…and I realized I must not die. *I'm not ready to die! They are not ready for me to die!*

I decided I would retreat again, returning down the tunnel, back the way I had come in. The ceiling was only inches above my head. All I could do was crawl backward, on my elbows, the tunnel floor pushing up my clothes, the rocks cutting into my skin. I could progress only in inches. I was hungry, now, and my mouth felt like leather coated with dust. I desperately needed a sip of water. I had to find the backpack—it was my only chance.

Beautiful images of my life, of Diane and Sophia and Jane, of family and friends, flashed past in rapid succession. But the images no longer gave me comfort; instead they goaded me into a deepening hysteria. They became more fleeting, ever dimmer, ever smaller….

I reached a point where a rocky protrusion from the ceiling blocked my way. I didn't remember seeing this rock, nor having to go around it. I could no longer trust my memory. I could not tolerate another obstacle. I had to get out! I could not die here! Desperation gave way to anger. I gave the rock a few powerful kicks with heel of my boot. I felt it give a little, which raised my spirits; and so I gave it one last fierce kick. It fell down, and suddenly I tasted dirt. I turned on the flashlight, and what I saw robbed me of all hope. I had dislodged a great rock, but now the tunnel had fallen in, blocking my only way back. At once my composure abandoned me. The truth of my situation burst fully into consciousness. I kicked the rock again and again in a blind fury. I raged against nature, against indifferent, immoveable necessity. I kicked until I cried out in pain—and I could kick no more. To compound my folly I had broken my ankle. I howled like a trapped animal, finally settling into low, spastic sobbing.

All is lost! Only now did I see it clearly. My family—all tenderness and warmth, all love and beauty, all memory—is lost. My children's beautiful faces, their smiles and tears, their passions, their future dreams—all were lost to me now. *Life is gone! And how did I spend it? On a "Great Goal" that has come to nothing! What folly, what stupidity!* I had squandered precious time, I poured precious life into the sand, all for a vain, selfish goal!

I was afraid to die alone. Cicero said philosophy is nothing but preparation for death. If that is so, then philosophy had failed me utterly. In no way was I ready. Now looking death in the eyes, I lost my nerve. I lashed out in desperation. *Don't let me struggle in fear and pain. Let me meet my end calmly!*

If only I had faith. But there was no God to listen to my pleas. The God of the Great Goal availed me not. I tried to prepare for my death. My mind wandered in terror....

> To the roots of the mountains I sank down;
> the earth barred me in forever.
> From deep in the realm of the dead I call for help....
>
> (Jonah 2, 1–7)

Why hadn't I been a better father, more selfless, more sympathetic, more dedicated to my kids? Why hadn't I been a better husband? I thought of Diane. I would never see her face again. Now the faces of everyone I had wronged or disappointed flashed by in rapid succession.

Please let me die in the light, in the warmth, in the tender embrace of my family! A lifetime of dammed-up tears now flowed powerfully, anointing my head for burial, dissolving me into the elements. At length my sobs diminished, became irregular and sporadic, then finally were quiet. The flashlight flickered and went black. My only hope now was for a quick death.

Chapter 23

Breakthrough

There is a story about the night Niagara Falls froze. The sudden silence was so profound that the townspeople woke up and ran outside. Silence arrived like a blow, reversing the polarity of their existence. They heard the ticking of the wall clock, and perhaps their own thoughts, for the first time.

Total darkness and silence fell on me like a bomb, exploding inwardly and obliterating every thought, every image from my mind. Darkness and silence came to life, began pulsing like a giant machine press, pounding me rhythmically into nothingness. Self-consciousness, affirming itself blindly, mechanically, again and again, was my only remaining thread to sanity. When that thread broke, I fell into the vastness of inner space. I was now a tiny seed, vanishingly small, a mere pip floating on an endless sea. Exposed to the infinite, "I" was erased.

For that reason this experience cannot be narrated in the first person. For there was no "I" remaining to narrate it.

Self-consciousness finally collapsed on itself, forming a black hole which devoured any remaining point of view, any possible self. Of course time and experience did not just stop. As to what happened next, the third person will be better suited to narrate it.

Peering into the infinity of inner space, a fearful void opened up, a void into which all thought and feeling, every dream and memory, and finally the last traces of the self, disappeared. But the loss of consciousness of all things and all beings did not leave nothing in its place. Rather, absent every object, including the self, there still remained a curious phenomenon: an awareness of something rather than nothing.[24]

For underlying existence is a field or fabric of energy called Being.Woven into this fabric, like warp to weft, is Non-Being. "Within Being, distinct yet inseparable from it, is Non-Being." [25] Being is a dynamic of opposed forces. Every being, every atom, every molecule, cell and creature participates in this dynamic. Death is inextricably part of life.

Ubiquitous but invisible, Being is paradoxically hidden among the plenitude and diversity of myriad beings. But it is periodically revealed by Non-being, for example by personal loss. Like that of King Lear, whose Truth only emerged after he had lost all things, and indeed all meaning.

Though it took billions of years, mind emerged from matter. Matter, finally understanding itself as mind, gains meaning and value. Mind, now grasping itself as matter, gains what it sought most—substance. Their difference is no longer tenable; the concept of objectivity and subjectivity is no longer sustainable. The spirituality of the concrete, and the concreteness of spirit, is now obvious.

> The earth is a living thing, the mountains speak. The trees sing. Lakes can think, pebbles have a soul, rocks have power.[26]

Spiritual phenomena are matter—of course! What else could they be? They are matter in a poorly understood form. If aggregates of neurons evolved over eons to produce stable, inheritable "states of mind," which eventually resulted in consciousness—is that so unlikely? If mind derived from a source *other* than matter, then matter and spirit would remain forever irreconcilable. We would always have two conflicting necessities, the objective and the subjective.

This intuition of Being presents a unitary subject and object. Each are infused with the qualities of the other in an exchange so complete that there is no longer "other." In this intuition not even death is "other." Being and Non-being are minutely entwined, just as "joy and woe are woven fine."[27] Intuiting one, we intuit the other. Every individual being enacts, in the struggle of existence, the eternal dynamic of Being and Non-being.

Chapter 24

Rebirth

I woke in a fetal position, shivering violently, my eyes tightly shut. Darkness and silence prevailed. Clearly death would not come quickly. I had lived well—but ultimately, I failed. I failed to create something great. I failed to leave the "legacy of memory" I wanted for my family. By dying foolishly, I had failed my family. I had failed to love them enough; I had failed to love life enough.

When my body is found, it will make a fitting picture of folly. *He went into a cave, the fool,* they'll say, *and could not find his way out. He tempted fate, the fool, spelunking alone. He lost his way and perished.* Folly and more folly. This is how I will be remembered, even by my loved ones.

My life was just thought now. There was nothing else to do. My body was numb, I had forgotten about it. By sheer force of habit I opened my eyes—and was stunned. I could *see* something.

Just inches above my face I saw a shadow, almost completely black, but not quite. Now, my eyes adjusting, I saw a saw a shape, I saw a line. Was I imagining it? Were my eyes actually open? I blinked a few times. Somewhere there was light! I dragged my frozen body forward on my elbows, every inch desperate and painful. Finally, advancing maybe ten feet, I craned my neck around a rocky mass and saw a needle-thin shaft of light shining down somehow from above. Driven by pure instinct now, I scraped and clawed toward the light.

A cat meowed. I thought, *I am imagining this. That can't be my cat, he never meows.* Certainly, I was deranged by hunger and thirst. Then came another meow, clear as day. "Bruno, Bruno," I called; but in place of my voice, I heard a hollow croaking sound in my head. My throat was parched, worthless. I couldn't speak. "Bruno, Bruno," I said in my head, my hands clawing painfully forward. The tiny thread of light was just ahead, only a few feet away. My hands were skinned, my nails broken. I pulled down the rocks and dirt blocking the light. A big rock fell down on my face, knocking me back and filling my mouth with dirt. The light was now just above me, but still I could not scream.

I heard a dog bark. *Juno!* Now I heard Diane: "Andrew! Where are you!" I reached forward, I put my last ounce of life into screaming: "Diiiiiii!" I croaked, inaudibly. This was my last chance. "Diiiiiiiiiiiiii!" Now the sound burst forth, exploding in my ears, echoing underground.

I stuck my finger into the gap where the light shone. I heard Diane scream "Oh my God!"—no doubt at the sight of a disembodied finger. Soon, I heard her moving rocks, opening the hole enough for me to put my hand through. For a time I could not hear her, only Juno and Bruno, raising hell in unison, barking and meowing continually. Then she came back with a shovel and crow bar. She pried loose a few big rocks, and soon I was out. I found myself, inexplicably, very close to where I had first entered the cave.

As the crushing weight of the world was lifted off me, I no longer heard Juno's barking or Diane's frantic cries. I lay on my side in the muddy crawlspace under the front porch as if it were the rarest luxury, as if I were basking on a beach. I was covered in mire, my hands were filthy and raw, my nails black, my face bloody and bruised, yet laying there all day would have been pure delight. Diane finally led me, by coaxing and pulling, out of the crawlspace, up the basement stairs, and into the kitchen. I drank a quart of water, and ate three bowls of Cheerios.

"Andrew! What happened!"

I was too unsteady to reply. I fell to my knees, clutching her legs for support. I closed my eyes and hoped it wasn't a dream….I was alive! I had another chance! Tears of joy streaked the dirt on my face. My chest heaved with sobs of relief. I collapsed on the kitchen floor.

At length, I gathered my wits, stood up, and looked carefully around me. Each thing glowed subtly, as if it were its own energy source. The coffee cup, the table, the lamp, the sink—each seemed precious, rich with meaning, and I wanted to remain with them. There was no intention or desire to draw me away. The fast moving clouds and waving trees outside caught my eye. I slid open the glass door and stepped onto the deck. Surveying the pond, forest, and stream, I was an organism returning to its natural setting.

Across the pond, the tops of the great white pines swayed in a hidden windstream; while the smaller trees beneath—the elms and maples, the brilliant white birches, mostly shorn of leaves, were still. The two burning bushes near the pond were brilliant orange and red. The deer had stripped the lower branches clean, conveying the impression of two torches. Two hawks flew over the treetops, exchanging shrill cries. Glancing downhill, to where the field meets the woods, two does stood stock-still, sensing my eyes upon them.

I know what to do now; I no longer require the threats and lashes of the will. I no longer required a motive. I thought of my goal and immediately turned back to the house. There was no longer a choice. I had to write. I limped indoors. Mounting the stairs, reaching the sunlit second floor landing, I felt lighter. I opened the door to the third floor stairwell. The whitewashed passage glowed from light pouring in through the skylight. I ascended slowly into an incandescent plasma. I sat down at the old-fashioned school desk to record the events of the last two days. For five hours I wrote, with no consideration of structure or style, the final chapters of the book.

When I finally came downstairs, I was not surprised to find that Diane had left, taking the pets in her friend's car, without a word. One look at the robotic determination in my eye, at my bloodied and mud-streaked face as I headed upstairs, was enough for her. Though she saved my life, she could see I was still hopelessly in thrall to the book. I had some serious explaining to do when I got back to the city. But when, sometime after nine o'clock, I got in my car to drive home, I had in my hands the finished manuscript. Finished, that is, but for one chapter.

Epilogue

I woke to the cries of seagulls, and then I remembered: Montauk. I drove here with my daughter Jane last night, struggling through the awful summer traffic on Fridays from Manhattan to the Hamptons. The traffic on the L.I.E. was an ordeal, bumper to bumper for more than two hours. Finally, near West Hampton, the traffic loosened up a little. Cars started to peel off of Route 27, turning toward their final destinations. Weekenders found their expensive seasonal homes, guests found their hosts, clubbers found their way to clubs. But we passed the Hamptons by, and still had another hour of driving. We were headed to the very tip of Long Island for one reason only: sharks.

Jane wanted to be a marine biologist. One day at dinner last year, she declared: "Dad, I want to study sharks." "Great," I said. "You know, the Baltimore Aquarium is not too far. They have a great exhibit of live sharks. Wanna go?" "No," she said. "I mean, up close." She typed a few words into her cell phone and showed me a video of giant schools of hammerheads in Costa Rica. "I want to see *this*."

I could hardly refuse. Jane was really into it. She saw the shark thriller *47 Meters Down* and wanted a closer look. Before long, we obtained our SCUBA certifications, then dove with manatees in Florida. Tomorrow, Jane would take another step toward her dream.

We arrived at the motel around midnight, and crashed immediately. Only a moment later, or so it seemed, I heard seagulls. An iPhone alarm ("Harp") sounded: 5:00 A.M.

"Jane! The sun is almost up! Get your gear together!"

She groans. My sixteen year old can effortlessly sleep until noon. I get coffee going in the little coffee maker on the desk, loading up on the powdered non-dairy creamer and sugar.

We lug our gear across the marina parking lot to the dock where our chartered boat is tied. We drop our gear, sit with our coffees, legs dangling over the end of the dock. The horizon glows and trembles in purple, then red, then yellow, and then just like that the sun was up. We shiver for a few more minutes, then head over to the diner for breakfast.

We'd been waiting for this day for a long time. We would dive a wreck (the *Grecian*, sunk near Block Island in 1932)—then, in the afternoon, we'd dive in the shark cage. We got lucky with the weather. A glassy sea, almost no wind. We booked a dive tour with an experienced crew and divemaster. But our stomachs were spidery with anticipation. I could tell Jane was nervous too.

"Ready?"

Jane nodded.

"I think we're totally ready, but I still have the jitters. What about you?"

"Not really, I'm okay," she said nonchalantly.

She was a very gutsy kid, but I think she felt better that I told her this.

An hour later we were on the boat, the *R/V Sea Turtle*, motoring slowly through the channel. Reaching the Sound, the boat accelerated. Anticipation rose and fell like the bow over the waves. We were surrounded by a diffused light, a cottony glow. The mist of salty air obscured the horizon; the sea and the sky seem to meet. I stood with Jane in the bow of the dive boat, the salty wind scrubbing our faces. Soon the *Sea Turtle* turned due east, directly into the rising sun.

With the engine at full throttle, we could no longer talk. My attention turned inward. There too I found a calm sea, its smooth surface reflecting the world above and the depths below. The great storm had passed. There was not a ripple, not a trace of the former turmoil.

For now I had broken the fever of the unfettered will. I had left it behind in the cave, like a deadly tropical disease. I had sweated out the urgency for change, the hunger for achievement, the lust for the goal. Goal-fever finally subsided and my vision cleared, revealing a higher value—helping *others* achieve their goals.

The captain throttled the engine—the wreck was just ahead. We unpacked our gear, suited up, and made our way slowly through the safety checklist. Each step, every detail had my total attention. My focus was on Jane, her equipment, her readiness, her feelings. No thought of yesterday or tomorrow. No thought of bloody achievement. All meaning, all value, was gathered before me now.

The first two divers in our group were ready to go. First one, then the other, rolled off the gunwale, dropping backward into the sea.

"Wanna go first?" Jane asked.

"Well...this is really your gig, why don't you go first?

She gave me an dubious look.

"I'll be right behind you," I added.

We sit on the gunwales, facing the deck. Jane gives her regulator one final test, then, taking it out of her mouth, shows a big smile. "Thanks, Dad." I smile and give her a double thumbs-up, and she rolls back gently into the sea.

Once she is settled in the water, I roll in, we exchange OK signs, then fall in together behind the divemaster.

Appendix A:

The Paradox Of Goals

(Extract from Miloš Janáček, *The Phenomenon of Choice.* [2007. Prague: Pragma.] Chapter 3.)

Great achievers are often depicted as radical individualists, struggling with and finally breaking the chains of convention. This is a staple of biographies, particularly those of artists, scientists and captains of industry. It is typified in *Apple Comput*er's "Think Different" ad campaign. There are many examples in fiction; *The Fountainhead* by Ayn Rand is typical.

Fitzcarraldo, the title and subject of Werner Herzog's 1982 film, is another example. In his mad quest to bring opera to the Amazonian jungle, Fitzcarraldo embodies the radical act of will. Such unique individuals seem to defy all precedent. Their creativity implies a freedom of thought, a freedom from constraint.

But against such romantic notions of freedom, as bodies among other physical bodies in the world, our actions, conscious or otherwise, are fully determined by physical laws. As Kant states:

> ...all the actions of man in the world of phenomena are determined by his empirical character, and the co-operative causes of nature. If, then, we could investigate all the phenomena of human volition to

> their lowest foundation in the mind, there would be no action which we could not anticipate with certainty, and recognize to be absolutely necessary from its preceding conditions. So far as relates to this empirical character, therefore, there can be no freedom.... [1]

Our bodies, from their grossest to their tiniest actions, must conform totally to physical laws. It follows that our deepest thoughts and desires are at bottom neuro-chemical processes, exhaustively determined by an unbroken series of prior physical causes.

Of course, we don't view our motives and goals this way at all. We don't regard them as physically caused. For inwardly it appears as though we are free to make choices, to affirm or deny, to accept or reject, or to go in another direction entirely. We seem to dictate our own direction. We direct our bodies to do things, as if *we* were the final cause of action. But universal laws state the opposite, namely, that all our thoughts and intentions are determined by an infinite regress of prior material causes. For if our thoughts were truly spontaneous and self-generating (*sui generis*)—in other words, had no antecedent—it would be truly miraculous, defying all physical law.

Is every thought and feeling without exception physically determined? Is every dream and goal traceable to a remote material cause? In the face of overwhelming physical, biological, and social influences on our behavior, could freedom still be possible?

---

1 Immanuel Kant, *Critique of Pure Reason,* trans. J.M.D Meiklejohn (New York: Colonial Press, 1899), 309

In what follows we will account for the most significant influences determining our will and choices, and then by a reductive method, reveal what ground—if any—remains for freedom to stand on. We will begin with individual goals, which have the unshakeable appearance of being consciously and freely chosen. How could a person's conscious, deliberate goals arise not by an act of free will but organically, out of nature and culture?

A. Natural Goals

The notion of "natural goals" is a paradoxical one. For we normally think of goals as something we choose, rather than something which is given or naturally occurring. But in fact our goals—despite the appearance of involving conscious choice—are largely predetermined by nature and convention.

As a matter of convention, we should distinguish between goals and purposes. The terms are often used interchangeably. A goal is an *intentional* end or purpose, proposed (initially) by an individual in a conscious and deliberate act. It is explicit, and though one can (and often does) adopt the goals of others, this adoption is also a conscious act, and a pledge to individual action.

But many purposes are not intentional, but what I will call *objective*. These are impersonal, external principles, which we are often unaware of, that determine our action toward unknown ends. Aristotle famously found purposes built into nature. Each thing has its own *telos*. The purpose of a seed is to become a plant or produce a flower; the purpose of an infant is to become an adult. Later naturalists regarded reproduction (the carrying forward of genes) as the primary purpose of any individual. But what is the purpose of reproduction? Evolution provides a mechanism explaining how species survive or perish. The "fittest" survive. But to what end? Is there a hidden purpose to evolution, for example to produce intelligent life? Is there any purpose to the larger phenomenon of life, whether on earth or elsewhere? If not, this is hard for humans to conceive. For where no purpose is found, we naturally imagine it and hope for it.

Putting aside the question of objective purposes, humans also possess an inner, subjective sense of purpose, which finds sufficient meaning in the objects of the world to operate within it. This sense of purpose undergirds and charges the will, giving it the strength to choose and act.

Thus goals are fundamentally different from those objective purposes in which we unwittingly participate (e.g., the purposes the body, the family, the economy, society, nation, human race, etc.). When we become consciously aware of these larger purposes, it is possible to then identify with them by intentionally choosing goals associated with them. By rendering our participation in larger purposes intentional, it can be made into an individual goal.

In any case, as a matter of convention, when a purpose derives from a conscious motive, we will call it a "goal"; when it derives from an external, impersonal force, we will call it a "purpose".

The life of a wildebeest conforms strictly to the laws of nature. The creature is moved by instinct, food, predators—by the struggle for survival. It cannot be said to have a goal, but only a purpose, given by nature through genes, natural selection, physical resources, climate, etc. Goals require intention, and the wildebeest intends nothing. He is moved directly by stimulus, such as hunger, fear, or whatever objects happen to appear before him. Other behaviors are determined by instinct. For example migration. The individual wildebeest is moved by nature's purposes, that is, by instinct, not by intention. These stimuli are not motives or mental representations that the wildebeest is free to choose or reject.

Like other animals, humans act by instinct; for example, in the care of their children. But we also deliberately choose to care for them. How does something *given* by nature become something *chosen* by an individual? How does a *purpose*—an end dictated by the demands of nature (e.g., a shelter) or by convention (e.g., marriage)—become a *goal,* a person's explicit, chosen intention? This paradox is the subject of this chapter. Since a goal requires a motive, how do nature's purposes enter the domain of consciousness in order to provide that motive, which then stimulates the person to deliberately, consciously undertake a goal?

Our earliest awareness of our family and social situation finds us in a world in which our goals are already underway. As Heidegger expressed it, we are thrown into a world with pre-existing rules and conditions. Similarly we "awaken" from states of mind in which the will had been suspended. Or we awaken from sleep, with a certain disposition or sense of purpose. Or we awaken from daydreams, from intense "spells" of work or play, from meditation, medication, moods, passions—and a goal appears.

One example of a natural goal is talent. Talent bestows on its recipient an implicit long-term goal at an early age. Talent is given, not made, and is often accompanied by a desire to use or express that talent. If a child plays ball and excels at it, they naturally wish to repeat the play (especially if they are praised by the parent) again and again. Talent provides a kind of built-in vocation. In its fulfillment is the promise of lasting satisfaction. In talent, the individual principle (motive) joins the external motivating principle (ability) with a powerful result.

B. Mythic goals

Myths produce goals today quite differently than in ancient times. The changing media of storytelling accounts for most of the change. If stories in those times were told exclusively around the tribal campfire by elders or shaman or poets, today storytelling is offered through very various and changing media and are in turn modified by them. The power of myth to inspire action has not diminished, but because of the internet and Marvel superhero film franchises, has only grown. (The mythic consciousness of our earliest ancestors was a primitive form of thought; in these post-rational times myth, especially in politics and commerce, threatens to do away with thought entirely. If the program of the enlightenment drove myth into exile, the latter has returned with a vengeance and turned the tables.)

Ancient stories of gods and heroes—the Epic of Gilgamesh, the Ramayana, the Bhagavad Gita, the twelve labors of Hercules, the seven labors of Rostam, the Iliad, the Odyssey, and others—inspired the heroism of countless generations. Heroic stories, in turn, spawned new myths, and new heroic imitators. Alexander the Great supposedly fashioned his ambition after the exploits of Hercules. Vico discovered,[2] Frazer documented,[3] and Eliade explained[4] the historic

---

2 Giambattista Vico, *The New Science,* trans. Thomas Bergin and Max Harrold Fisch, (Ithaca: Cornell University Press, 1948)

3 Sir George Frazer, *The Golden Bough: A Study in Magic and Religion,* (Oxford: Oxford University Press, 1994)

4 Mircea Eliade, *Sacred and Profane: The Nature of Religion,* trans. Willard Trask. (New York: Harcourt, 1987.)

ground of mythic consciousness. Myth presents behaviors to emulate, to imitate—it generates motives and inspires action. Myths generate goals. Indeed, myth is more a source of culture than a product of it.

Mythic goals are like natural goals, in that they are first pursued unreflectively. However, unlike natural goals, which move the body directly, myths move the body only indirectly, through images and stories. The hero's actions are encoded in the myth. The myth is not just a story, but a script. Through the retelling of the shaman, priest or elder, the ancestor transmits the script to the young hero. The boldest in each generation are moved, without thought or reflection, to heroic acts by the boldness of their ancestors. Thus mythic goals are passed on through successive generations.

A god or mythical ancestor animated those early heroes through *mimesis.* But when, at a later period in human history, the hero became capable of reflecting on his intentions, he came to realize that the myth he is re-enacting, the story he is living, is actually *his own* goal. Until that point, the hero acted directly at the behest of culture (through the imagination) not by an individual principle of the will. Once the story he is enacting becomes an idea he can grasp as his own, i.e., as an object of his will, it is no longer a mythic "purpose" but an individual goal. Once the goal embedded in the myth is posited as the hero's own intention, it becomes a goal proper—*his* goal. Countless generations must have passed before the principle of action passed from the natural purpose embedded in the myth to an individual goal, i.e., an act of will with a motive, an act the hero recognizes as his own.

The power of myth did not disappear with archaic man. It is vibrantly alive in early childhood, as Vico first noted, forming our earliest motives and actions. Its power is well known to Hollywood directors and Madison Avenue executives. They understand the deep reserves of motivation that myth taps into. Young boys are especially possessed, it seems, tirelessly re-enacting the superhero's exploits. As the steady stream of comic book superhero films attest, myth has universal cultural resonance and appeal.

C. Conventional Goals

Humans are natural mimics. We willingly follow customs, and mimic conventions, in exchange for acceptance and security. In early childhood, when we first become aware of our social situation, we find that family and community goals have already been assigned to us, if only tacitly. They are given to us purely by convention, well in advance of our understanding or approval. Education, employment, marriage, family, social position are the obvious examples. Social behaviors—and desirable social outcomes—are continuously reinforced by its members through imitation and conformism.

In fact most goals, if we are to be honest, are determined by convention. I mean *convention* in the broadest sense, which includes any myth, custom, artifact, art, law, tool, institution, thought, invention or product devised by man. We find comfort in conformity. That is why, as Vico says, conventions are upheld more effectively by custom than by law.[4] Force creates resistance, while custom creates pleasure insofar as it is willingly followed. Indeed, it might be said that a culture's purpose is to produce a compelling, fundamentally unquestioned, sustainable way of life.

We unreflectively adopt the goals of family, friends, corporations, and nations as our own. Collectively, these "programs" consume much of our waking lives. From our individual perspective, we leverage both nature and convention to attain our personal goals. But from a larger perspective, we are the instruments of nature and convention. From our individual perspective, we have chosen; but from the wider perspective of natural and social purposes, we have *been* chosen. Nevertheless, the individual must resist, from time to time, the natural and social purposes that control him, and insist on his individual goals instead.

By the time in early childhood when we become self-aware, we are already pursuing natural, mythic, and conventional goals. Self-consciousness arises in a pre-configured environment. It is "thrown into the world,"[5] finding sets of values, expectations, and requisite actions pre-fabricated and ready to use. Family and community voices incessantly repeat those values: get good grades, go to college, become a doctor, get married, etc. Many—probably most—of our goals are in this way "given" to us.

Heidegger's concept of "thrownness" (*Geworfenheit*)—describes the experience of "falling" into a world—or into a state of mind, a mood, a role—or a goal. Even the most driven and accomplished individuals—with a wall of degrees, a corner office, successful by any measure—sometimes must wonder how they got there. In a rare moment of insight they reflect: "This is not my beautiful house…this is not by beautiful wife."[6] One reason for the disconnect? Despite their real efforts, convention did most of the work.

---

5 Martin Heidegger *Being and Time, trans.* John Macquarrie and Edward Robinson (New York, Harper & Row, 1962.) Page 466.

6 David Byrne and Brian Eno, "Once in a Lifetime" On *Remain in Light.* (New York: Warner Music Group, 1981)

D. Rational Goals

Certain events or states of mind can make us reflect on our lives and its overall meaning. Some examples: the death of a loved one, moments of great regret, moments of deep self-doubt, moments of failure. Such events and subsequent states of mind reflect our lives as a whole into one picture-frame, so to speak. It may happen at that moment, typically in adolescence, when children first critique their parents (whether overtly or silently). Parents represent, and indeed are, powerful forces of convention and it is natural for a child to reinforce their ego by defining themselves negatively, in opposition to their parents. At a minimum, a teenager does not want to be like their parents in this or that way. In this "critique", whether implicit or explicit, adolescents grasp their parents' lives for the first time in an objective way, as a whole; thus reflecting back a vision of their own lives, taken as whole, opening up before them.

Rational goals assert freedom from convention or other influences. For reason and logic provides a true basis for judgement, not relying on received wisdom, custom, opinion or myth. Rational goals are conscious, deliberate, appear to be freely chosen, and further seem to present a standard for action. Reason's mission, announced in the Enlightenment, was to correct the inequities of nature, ignorance, bias, the illusions of religion, the ravages of tyranny, arbitrary power, social injustice, the falsities of convention.

Reason's fundamental contribution to goal-setting is the attribution of goals to free choice. Rather than accept the hand that fate has dealt us, reason asserts that we may freely determine our lives with goals. Reason is inclined to think it determines the course of goals, and life, more than it truly does.

Reason is under the spell of wrong attribution, the belief in the free will. That said, belief in the importance and the possibilities of reason profoundly affects the world.

For our purposes, the term "rational goal" does not signify a goal that satisfies logical scrutiny. Instead, it designates goals which are self-conscious and considered justifiable.

E. Personal Goals

What if we reject the goals we find ourselves "thrown" into, the goals that culture and convention offer to us, or worse, require of us? What if we lack a talent or vocation, or even strong inclinations? What if we don't want to get married or have a family, or follow the other scripts that society has written for us? Where will we find purpose, if not in the goals that have been foisted upon us by convention? Or, no less likely, what if we have adopted those conventional goals and succeeded in conventional terms, but still find no satisfaction in them? Personal goals offer the possibility of fulfillment through one's own efforts alone. They offer an independent source of meaning and purpose that does not depend on "given" goals. Even if we are a "failure" in conventional terms, we can turn to our Personal goals and find meaning and purpose therein.

Personal goals are either outwardly or inwardly directed. *Outward* personal goals seek to change the external conditions of our lives. I'd like to lose ten pounds, move to a nicer neighborhood, get a better job, etc. *Inward* personal goals, in contrast, seek to effect change in inner life. I'd like to be more patient and considerate of others. I'd like to have more willpower and discipline, to be more organized, more thorough. I'd like to be able to effect inner change. Personal goals are often self-improvement projects, which have the net effect of fortifying the ego.

Personal goals appear to the goal setter to be freely and consciously chosen, in contrast to the demands of private and professional life, which appear to be conscious and intentional, but hardly free. Whereas a new initiative, a deliberately chosen, purely positive personal undertaking, looks like the opposite, the very definition of free will. The goal setter's intentions appear to be the cause of the goal.

Personal goals provide a hedge against the loss of meaning that sometimes results from a lifetime of Conventional goals. Should we fail at Conventional goals, or succeed but find no satisfaction in them, Personal goals offer a source of meaning and purpose independent of convention.

Humans naturally desire and envision improvement. We envision a better immediate outward state for ourselves (e.g., home, profession, family, community); we also envision a better inward state (peace, happiness, wisdom, etc.). These desires, combined with intentionality (our power to focus on and acquire objects), give rise to Personal goals focusing on outward objects or inward states.

Inward Personal goals reveal our capacity for self-knowledge and self-mastery. They also provide a hedge for Outward personal goals, should they exhaust our money. For self-knowledge and self-control are far greater and more lasting abilities than the value of most, if not all objects.

F. Great Goals

In the course of one's life a Great Goal may appear, perhaps unaccountably, perhaps unbidden. It might not be recognized initially as such. For it hails from the unconscious, and its hidden aim is to transcend the ego. This is not clear at the outset and may never be fully grasped by the goal setter. Great Goals will however be recognized by a few common traits. The first quality, *magnitude,* is suggested by its name. The Great Goal seeker wants to become larger or part of something larger. This is not narcissism, but an innate, unconscious yearning for growth, expressed initially as the expansion of the ego.

Great Goals have a related quality: *ultimacy.* The seeker feels constrained by his conventional self. He feels oppressed by feelings of smallness, of narrowness. He has an urgent — if unconscious—desire to break free the shackles of his limiting self-view. He strives instinctively to find his limits, to test them and break through them.

Another quality of Great Goals is the yearning for *transformation*. The seeker yearns inwardly for change and sees the goal as something that will change him. The seeker imagines, if only vaguely, the transformed self that will appear when the goal is achieved.

But the most notable trait of the Great Goal is that it feels *subjectively necessary.* This sense of necessity might seize the seeker with a passion, like love at first sight. But more often it takes root slowly and secretly, unconsciously overcoming all doubts and resistance, gradually becoming inwardly necessary, thereby ensuring unqualified commitment from the seeker. A Great Goal always originates from within, and if it takes hold becomes an imperative, despite outward pressures or inward fears.

A Great Goal is not pursued for personal gain, aggrandizement or advantage. Its value to the seeker must be intrisic and self-justifying, an end in itself. If it is instead merely a means to an end, it is not a Great Goal, but perhaps just a great

Personal goal. In any case, by the time the seeker consciously feels the necessity of the goal, his identity has been imprinted on it. It has become a vital source of meaning, such that failure at the Goal will be a failure of identity. Given this risk, a Great Goal has the highest possible stakes.

This sense of inner necessity may first express itself in feelings of constraint, discontentment with our progress, impatience with our limitations, a desire for insight, a yearning for change, a yearning to overcome our alienation from ourselves, from others, from the world. A Great Goal might take a purely introspective form, such as striving for a breakthrough in meditation, or writing a memoir, or learning to live with the loss of a loved one. But very often the goal is external, something visible, tangible, perhaps impressive. For it is natural to imagine that our greatest potential for achievement lies in external objects. Climbing Everest, creating a work of art, organizing a political movement, starting a philanthropy: on the face of it these are impressive goals; but if they are Great Goals, they arise from a deep inner need, for example the desire to test one's mental and physical limits, or the desire to confront fear and self-doubt. A marathon has a grueling physical aspect, but has an equally grueling psychological aspect: rigor, discipline, self-denial. The Great Goal reveals our limits, and by direct implication our final limit, death.

Great Goals arise not from conscious motives, outward experience, social pressures or chance; but rather from the depths of inner life. Though seen by the seeker himself as a conscious, concrete goal, it in fact arises from the necessity of unconscious striving for a higher spiritual form. It is not driven by outward social influences; it is not attempted because of outcomes or consequences; it is undertaken because it feels inwardly *necessary*. Beyond our reasons and justifications, a

Great Goal feels totally valid and justified in itself. Ultimately the seeker will not need reasons, justifications, habits or other props to achieve his Great Goal. Based on the sense of subjective necessity alone, he will eventually commit to it unconditionally, such that willpower and conscious effort are no longer required.

Personal goals express the natural human tendency toward self-improvement, by which we gradually fortify the ego, layer by layer, against threats that would undermine it. The ego includes not only thoughts, feelings and experiences, but also one's body, possessions, family, friends, community, social commitments and judgements. By regular efforts we fortify the ego with experiences and improvements, with discipline and achievements, with knowledge and training. The more outwardly impressive the conventional self becomes (for example through possessions, prominence and power), the more it has to lose in reputation or social standing should it be undermined or threatened. Thus the ego tends to be conservative, preferring change—if any—that is incremental, not radical.

If Personal goals strengthen the ego, Great Goals put it at risk. As the foundation of the seekers' status quo, the ego is an obstacle that must be overthrown. In Great physical goals, like the proverbial scaling of Everest, the willingness to risk one's life is merely the outward expression of this inward need. It is ready to risk the ultimate loss: outwardly the loss of the body; inwardly, the loss of the self. For this reason the seeker may stake all to achieve his Great Goal. He will sacrifice comfort, complacency, reputation; he will put his chances for happiness at risk. The Great Goal does not build up the self, but on the contrary spends it, exhausts our deepest resources to find its limits. It expresses the human need to go beyond oneself.

The inner self yearns for its next phase of growth. The Great Goal is a vehicle for that growth. Like the butterfly trying its wings against the chrysalis, the pressure of inner growth is just as pressing and urgent as the next phase of physical development. The desire to achieve something great is not egoism or megalomania. Rather, it expresses a deep, unconscious yearning for spiritual breakhrough. To reach it, more effort, more willpower, more struggle and strife will not avail. It requires abandoning the former self. As the butterfly sheds the chrysalis, the binding, limiting ego must fall away to let a higher self emerge. But the comfort of the familiar, and anxiety about the unknown, often hold us back.

The desire to make a mark—to make a lasting impression on the world—is not a purely conventional impulse, as is generally supposed. Instead, the attempt to make an indelible mark—the Great Goal—is an eruption of inner growth which, in its upper reaches, overcomes the self's identification with the body and the ego. The desire to create something lasting is no different from the Hero's desire for immortality.

Psychologically, the Great Goal can be regarded as a "denial of death"— a denial of one's limits, of mortality, of finality. We unconsciously deny the necessity of death by asserting our own, subjective necessity: freedom. But the Great Goal is more than a denial of death—for it is an active engagement with it. The seeker, grappling with Death in the guise of the Great Goal, transforms it from an opaque, paralyzing force into something concrete with which we can engage. Only by grappling with Death can we look it in the eye and begin to neutralize its terrifying power. This engagement is perhaps more of a dance than a wrestling match. For we may take action and fearlessly lead, or passively wait, and fearfully follow. We alternate between the two postures of engagement and anxiety. From a distance, in the anticipation of contact, the anxiety of death reaches a maximum—but is instantly discharged once the dance begins.

Natural, mythic, and conventional goals are "given" to every goal-seeker. They precede our awareness, they operate largely on the level of the unconscious. They condition and determine our thoughts and actions on a fundamental level. But with the advent of reason, given goals may no longer be accepted. What is given – in other words, necessity – is regarded as hostile to reason and freedom. Henceforth reason would examine and justify all goals. Thus reason came to take "justifiable" goals as the standard for all others.

In contrast to Rational goals, in the Great Goal we first witness the operations of necessity—inwardly in our thoughts and outwardly in our actions—*but do not resist.* In a Great Goal, we move past the understanding of necessity as a purely external force. For the experience of subjective necessity enables the seeker to not merely identify with, but positively affirm external necessity. We choose necessity as if it were our own. In pursuit of a Great Goal we still suffer our fate, as its unwitting agent; but we also deliberately choose and participate in it. This wisdom has a name: *Amor Fati,* love of fate.

Appendix B:

What Is Character?

(Extract from Miloš Janáček, *Reach for Greatness.* [2013. New York: Harper Torchbooks.] Chapter 8.)

A. Introduction

In the throes of catastrophic failure, the seeker is at the mercy of events. His ship, tossed violently on towering seas, is foundering. The end is at hand. With no way forward, and no other recourse, he lowers anchor. He seeks bedrock—something unshakeable, beyond question. Finally the anchor finds the hard bottom of his nature—character. Character alone can save him from this fatal drift, because it contains within it a deep and unquestioned principle of action. Character produces the *subjective necessity* to act. Even after the self is overwhelmed and swept away, character still declares unequivocally what the seeker *must* do. When reason, experience, and hope fail, character must lead the way.

But first he must grasp that he has failed. Passive failure—a mere drifting away from the scene of failure, or running full-tilt away from it—offers no insight into character. But true failure—*failure proper*—reveals all. It is the full acknowledgement and acceptance of failure. With failure proper, the seeker "takes ownership" of failure. He takes failure "upon himself".[7] Ownership of failure reveals character—not to oth-

7 Paul Tillich, *The Courage to Be.* (New Haven: Yale University Press, 1952.)

ers perhaps, but to the seeker himself. This chapter explores the relationship between failure and character.

"Objectively", we might attribute our own failure to many things. We might blame it on events, on timing, on others. If we were strict determinists, we would say our failure was necessary, it *had* to happen. But when, conversely, we take full responsibility for our failure—when, despite the myriad causes beyond our control, we embrace them as our own—the subject declares its *own* necessity. By taking responsibility for outcomes beyond our control, the subject assert its agency and freedom.

The old chestnut that 'failure builds character" turns out to be true. But before "building" starts, prior structures must fall. When that goal on which everything depends—in which everything is invested—comes crashing down to the foundations, then *failure proper* reveals the bedrock of character that lies beneath.

B. What Is Character?

Character must first be distinguished from personality. Visible traits like expressions, behaviors, tendencies, aversions, moods, temperament—we usually associate with personality. Personality is typically understood as largely genetic, given by nature, unchangeable. One is not responsible for one's personality. On the other hand, many character traits such as honesty, humility, loyalty, etc., are regarded as deep but still changeable. Character can be improved. Certainly that is the opinion of all moralists (if not all psychologists).

We are rightly judged by what we can control or affect, rather than by what we have no ability to change. The common understanding is that one does not have to be a jerk.

One can correct their jerkiness. One could act otherwise; one could be fairer, more thoughtful; one could have made better choices. Fairness is a moral character trait, which is to say it can be modified and improved. In effect, it is commonly believed—and criminal law presumes—that one can be good if one wishes.

First we will consider outward character, often called personality, and then inward character, which has two parts: moral character, and mental character.

Character sometimes refers to the essential qualities of a thing. For example, the character of diamond is clear hard carbon. The character of coal is soft black carbon. What is the character of a human? *Homo sapiens* is a creature of nature, but aware of itself as distinct and apart from nature. It is also simultaneously a part of and separate from its social world. Though *Homo sapiens* is a social animal, the individual often insists on its needs over and against the needs of society. *Homo sapiens* is further divided inwardly, because self-consciousness persistently separates him even from himself. Thus *Homo sapiens* has, irreduceably, an outward and an inward character.

C. Outward Character

Are we fastidious or sloppy, organized or scatterbrained, loud or quiet? Are we punctual or late, energetic or lethargic, engaged or detached, serious or humorous, passionate or cool? What preferences, aversions and reactions do we consistently show to others? This is outward character, otherwise known as personality. These traits are visible, persistent and easy to recognize.

The original meaning of the Greek word character (Χαρακτήρα) is *inscription* (e.g., an impression/letter/number/

picture/symbol in clay/stone/parchment, etc.) A character is a mark of some kind. Among the flora and fauna of nature, these marks are visible traits and behaviors. The late nineteenth century pseudoscience phrenology attempted to determine human character purely from outward marks, particularly the shape of the head and facial features. Phrenology did not survive the scrutiny of the advancing sciences of neurology and psychology, but retained its adherents far longer than it should have—not despite, but because of its racist overtones. As late as 1920 respected authors published books on phrenology, for example Hamilton McCormick's *Characterology,* which described the "science" of determining human character by outward marks alone.

Around this time modern psychologists, beginning seriously with Jung, proposed various frameworks for personality typing. These are based on the classification of behavioral traits, such as introversion and extroversion, in addition to direct feedback from patients in analysis, including written assessments about preferences, aversions, fears, interests, etc. Aggregates of observable traits and behaviors (e.g., friendliness, passivity, etc.) are related to different personality types.

The ability to read personality types, sometimes called character judgement, may provide an evolutionary advantage. The first hominins who grasped the rules predicting the behavior of others would likely live longer to transmit their genes. The ability to "size up" a stranger as opponent or friend is an advantage. An example is the con artist. They are quick judges of character. They deftly size up their dupes; they exploit the knowledge of type for gain. If character types are a product of natural selection, then certainly some character types, under different environmental conditions, would have perpetuated their genes more successfully than others.

The majority of Fortune 500 companies use personality assessment tools such as Myers-Briggs and DiSC. Managers want to determine in advance, as much as possible, the applicant's suitability to the job; what motivates them; how well they interact with others; etc. In effect, a manager wants to predict an applicant or employees' behavior as much as possible. They want to see if their character comports with institutional norms. How will they handle conflict? How will they handle pressure? Are they management material? Underlying these tests is, necessarily, a theory of character. Whether or not character assessment is—or can ever become—"scientific", the Myers-Briggs and DiSC companies, and their myriad customers, presume the existence of character types.

D. Inner Character

Just as evolution worked over millennia to form outward character, it also, by variation and mutation, developed inward character. In other words, it developed a collection of stable mental states, varying by individual, which includes standard variations (stable sub-states such as the receptive state, the productive state, the willful state, the creative state, the playful state, etc.). This component of inner character is called mental character. The biological structure (or morphology) of steady states of mind is one way of looking at inner character "objectively". Objectively, this would be a nexus of nerve cells in regular, perhaps continuous, communication, in the form of a robust pattern of electro-chemical pulses. This, or something like it, would be required to produce a steady state of mind, in other words, a reliable set of mental responses, to which deranged or unsettled states eventually return. A steady default state of mind would have undeniable evolutionary value. For this reason it is natural to infer that some mental states are heritable. An unstable mind puts its bearer at a disadvantage and society at risk. This was no less true in Neolithic times than today. Certain human and social capacities (for example, the attainment of long-term goals) rely heavily on dependable, consistent mental states. One consequence of steady, heritable mental states is culture.

As the human form has five senses, there are also five mental structures, by which we register inward impressions: perception, emotion, imagination, intellect and will. The influence that each of these powers wields in the psyche, relative to the other powers, varies in each individual. This results in different default states of mind for each mental character type. Balances and imbalances between the faculties, and the mental states these produce, have a distinct effect on motivation, decision making, and action which will be explored further below.

Just as we can't account for the idiosyncrasies of our personality, we likewise can't explain why we are, for example, emotionally cool but warmly receptive to physical sensations; or why we are emotionally warm but intellectually cool and analytical. These are "mental" character traits.

When discussing the mental faculties, any language suggesting they are things, rather than dynamic processes, must be avoided. It is easy, perhaps natural to "reify" or make an object out of these active processes by thinking of them as "organs". In any case, cursory inward examination suggests nothing like distinct organs. Rather, it shows, in any given mental representation, all powers together, interwoven and vibrating in unison like guitar strings. Their functions are generally harmonious but occasionally quite dissonant, compromising the effectiveness of not merely the psyche but also the person.

The examination of inner character cannot be conducted empirically. Rather it is conducted through introspection. By direct inward seeing, the outputs of the five powers—sense perceptions, images, feelings, ideas and intentions—are easily discerned. If we close our eyes, the chair we are sitting in, the warmth of the room, etc., are regarded inwardly as perceptions. Looking at the continuously changing images and forms crossing our minds, from the outrageous to the banal, we see the activity of the imagination. If we feel delight or dread or both for no apparent reason, we know the emotions are active and healthy. A moment spent thinking about the size or shape of something, an arrival time, or the profitability of an investment, assures us that our intellect is functional. Now and again an image reappears that reliably grips the heart. Perhaps it is following through on a promise you made to yourself. Maybe the house you want to buy one day; or a professional achievement you have been working on for years; or the marathon you plan to run next year. These images instantly remind us that we must act. And now we know the will is alive and strong, cracking the whip, pushing you to your goals.

As we observe our changing inner state, as fascinating as the contents of each faculty is, in order to understand mental character we must focus on the dynamic interaction between the mental faculties, i.e., on our overall mental state.

E. Moral Character

What is moral character? It appears to be an inherent mental trait of *Homo sapiens* with a very specific function. Moral character acts, reflexively, based on values. Moral character is not the source of values; rather, moral character preserves, upholds and defends the values that have been learned through experience. Because some values are innate and others are learned, they vary widely. Which means that moral character, in the preservation or defense of such numerous and different values, determines a wide range of actions and behaviors.

We can define moral character in a purely functional way. Its apparent biological function is to enable reflexive action based purely on values. Moral character short-circuits decision-making, bypassing the frontal lobe where conscious choices are made, and in defense of a specific value initiates a program of action without further ado. Our core values are so fundamental and ingrained that challenges to them elicit immediate responses, bypassing the higher brain and executing a program of action. But moral character is not merely defensive, but also an active *upholder and promotor* of values, giving rise to an even wider variety of predetermined behaviors.

The guidelines for action that are embedded in moral character by means of values, relieves the higher brain of confusion and deliberation, and also produces more consistent results. Moral character provides a far more effective response to moral dilemmas than the labors of the intellect ever could. Moreover moral character can be used to produce reliable sets of actions and reactions to control mass movements—for example, by inculcating certain values, and conditioned responses, into soldiers and athletes by rigorous training. Values produce consistent action much more effectively than mere ideas.

Moral character has a second distinctive quality. It produces a sense of responsibility in its bearer, for the values it contains. Like a mother hen protecting her brood, moral character nurtures and defends the values under its custody. A value is in effect a "moral character trait" that the agent feels personally responsible for. Because we believe we are *free* to be honest or trustworthy (for example) we feel *responsible* to do so. To put it differently, when we regret our actions, it's because we believe we could have acted otherwise.

We don't feel responsible for our nervous tics, how we laugh, if we are reserved or anxious or excitable. For these are personality traits, naturally given and immutable. But as to whether we are generous, or kind, or loyal—we believe we have a choice. In other words we feel responsible for these traits. Through our moral character traits, we implicitly affirm our freedom.

Moral character traits are basically social virtues, given not by nature but by culture. Courage, generosity, temperance, modesty, etc. are selfless traits, placing the interests of society over those of the individual. The survival of our species depended more, perhaps, on fit societies than on fit individuals. But it depended above all upon human adaptability. Moral character is a triumph of adaptation. Moral character allows a young child, independent of race or ethnicity, to adapt to any human society and its values.

Though the substrate or core functions of moral character are innate, many different individual values are acquired or installed into this substrate during the course of a lifetime. As it is populated with values from birth, moral character, entirely without reflection, builds a valid playbook or set of default actions for when values are challenged. Values are, in effect, pre-rational principles of action, transmitted from generation to generation by stories, examples, maxims and warnings, and thereby inculcated into the moral character of children. Moral character reliably turns learned values into reflexive actions.

Values are not all positive or shining examples of selflessness. Some people value control of other people, which may lead directly to violence as a default way of resolving disagreements. Some people value the exclusion of other people, which may lead directly to bigotry and xenophobic behavior. Of course, these values and behaviors may not be considered "bad" in some cultures. Moral character contains no inherent goodness. The goodness of a person depends on the values that were instilled in their moral character.

It is conceivable that character corresponds to a lower-brain structure (clusters or networks of neurons, as yet unknown) that allows the body to act reflexively, unthinkingly, based on stored values. Certain deep values, though acquired, are unvaryingly upheld. A child, unobserved by others, sees money fall from her neighbor's pocket, and without a thought takes pains to return it. Her moral character has already been formed by her parents, community, and environment.

Character is a *hybrid* mental form consisting of "hardware" and "software". Though it is for the most part hardware (neurons, axons, ganglia, etc.), it also has a modifiable instruction set, akin to software. The modifiable part of character is the moral character, and its stored values are akin to software programs.

Moral character represents a novelty of human evolutionary adaptation. In ancient times, shaman, tribal leaders, and storytellers inculcated values through stories, not reason. For reason was feeble in the dawn of humanity, and abstractions could have little sway. By the imitation of the action in those stories (stored as values) immediately and without reflection, the individual would be guided in doubtful situations where instinct had no ready response.

The modifiability of moral character presents several adaptive advantages to our species. It is conceivably an improvement upon earlier fixed, or more rigid, mental qualities, allowing for better adaptation to an environment and its conditions. Moral character allows for customization, correction and improvement of an individual organism, to the end of self-preservation.

The values that take root in moral character during childhood strike deep. Uprooting them or changing them is a difficult and slow process, but possible. In fact people's values naturally change over the course of their lives.

F. Mental Character

Moral character does not operate in a vacuum, but interacts with the other mental faculties. This is noticeable in certain states of mind. In a rage, for example, we are not inclined to generosity, or humility, or any of the moral traits, for that matter. In a willful state, when all other considerations are cast aside to attain our goal, our ability to prioritize others is seriously compromised. In an intellectual state of mind—where the standards are logic and reason—sympathy and compassion may suffer. Our ability to access our moral character at any given moment is hindered, or facilitated, by different states of mind.

To moderate the wild vagaries of the mental state, evolution has, it seems, created a state of equilibrium between the mental faculties, a "default" mental state, which I call the *status animus*. This is a baseline or "resting" state, a "homeostasis" for the dynamically interacting mental powers (perception, emotion, imagination, intellect and will). In this baseline state, the weight and distribution of the mental powers vary with each person, but the baseline nevertheless exists for each.

Over great expanses of time variation, mutation and the crucible of natural selection produced a number of stable mental states. Variants (or regular combinations) of these proto-mental states became the basis for character types. Some character types might have superior adaptive value for the individual, while others may have superior adaptive value for the species.

F. The *Status Animus*

(a) Objective/Analytic view

The default mental state is defined differently depending on whether it is viewed objectively/analytically or subjectively/intuitively. Just as the human body has a *homeostasis*—the equilibrium of vital processes, such as heart rate, blood pressure, breathing rate, in a resting state —the psyche also has a default, steady physical state called the *status animus*. It is an equilibrium of the mental powers, to which all mental highs, lows, and other derangements eventually return. Certain human capacities (for example, long-term planning, or large-scale projects) depend heavily on a reliable, predictable mental state. The *status animus* would be advantageous to individual adaptation and thereby to the survival of the species. This is as true today as in Neolithic times.

From the standpoint of the understanding, the *status animus* is a concept, i.e., an abstract notion of forces dynamically interacting within a whole. It describes the influence of each power relative to the others and to the whole psyche, in the resting state. By attempting to measure this, we convert the immediate experience of the continuously changing and interpenetrating forces of the psyche, into "relative values" that can be expressed quantitatively, at a moment in time, as proportions, i.e., as numbers. This "standard configuration" of the powers provides a basis for character types.

Different character types might have been more successful at different stages of human history. Mutation would eventually produce novel character types, some of which would become especially successful or dominant, depending on the challenges of the time. (Nietzsche and Kierkegaard independently presented the figure of Socrates as a new character type—a rational type, or destroyer of conventions.) There is rich comic potential in character types that did not survive natural selection. Even fully aware of the physical, biological, and social forces determining our actions, we are nevertheless compelled to believe that our actions are driven by inner causes, like choice and motive. We can't help regarding ourselves as a subject or ego that "has" —i.e., is the source of—thoughts, feelings, and intentions. We see the connection between intent and action and we naturally assign causality to intent. Intentions appear to be the product of the conscious mind because they are only noticed in a conscious state. Of course, as Freud showed, consciousness represents only a fraction of the psyche's total activity. Like an iceberg, the greater part of the psyche's activity is beneath the surface, in the unconscious. Unless we are examining the psyche as a psychologist or psychoanalyst; or sunk deeply in introspection, we are generally unaware of the interaction of the faculties behind the scenes.

Though the fountain of inner appearances seems truly *sui generis,* they do not appear out of nothing. They are the product of the faculties—perception, emotion, imagination, understanding, and will—working in concert, and sometimes in conflict. In any action by any of the powers, the influence of the others is inextricably entwined. The faculties in their interaction condition all experience, based on their form.

Kant taught that space, time, and causality are inherent in the structure of the mind. To use Kantian language, they are the *a priori* conditions of any experience whatever. But these conditions of experience are purely formal; they have no content. Within the grand architecture of space and time, the faculties fill in the content. They assume a more prosaic role, akin to carpentry. By filling in the general forms of space and time with matter, texture, color, emotion, feeling, etc., the faculties dynamically generate the objective world, in real time, as it were. There may be forms of consciousness that contradict or negate all experience—for example a religious epiphany. But even that experience is inescapably shaped by the faculties, for otherwise, it could not register as an experience at all.

In each individual psyche, the dynamic interaction of the mental powers is not unique or arbitrary, but governed by laws. One law is the *status animus,* an individual's "default" or resting state of mind, to which the five psychic powers return after regular departures from it. For example, at work we push our team to meet a critical project deadline. An intensity of will is needed to meet this goal, relative to our default willfullness as represented in the status *animus.* This willful state may persist, or even build to a point where the will becomes dominant in the personality, effectively sidelining other faculties. But eventually the headstrong will must return to its proper place as one power among many in a cooperative dynamic. Perhaps over the weekend we visit several art galleries, go to the theater in the evening and a party after that. Sense perception has been overworked (relative to the optimal, as expressed by the *status animus).* And yet, for a different psyche, this much stimulus would have been insufficient. We watch an emotionally draining film, then have a terrible argument with an estranged sibling. By the end of the day, we are rendered emotionally numb and unavailable. Our emotions are overtaxed, in comparison with the optimal. Our emotional heights or intensities will eventually return to their normal state, as one power among many in a cooperative—and sometimes competitive—dynamic.

In the course of inner life, one faculty or another may come to dominate the psyche before returning (whether moments or years later) to the *status animus.* Immersed in the pleasures of sense, in the depths of emotion, in flights of imagination, compelled by burning ideas, or pangs of desire— it sometimes happens that a hyperactive faculty, in a kind of mania, resists the return to the status animus and instead attempts to retain control of the psyche. One power may unilaterally commandeer the psyche to the detriment of the person and society. An unyielding will meets disappointment more often than greatness; a powerful imagination produces more idlers than artists; a keen intellect produces more cynics than scientists. The disproportional gift—or curse—of a single dominant mental power, may drive a person to idleness, greatness or madness, but by this means evolution systematically ensures that each human possibility has been tried.

The capacities of the five mental powers vary widely among humans. When attempting to determine inner character, more important than capacity is the relative strength of each power in an individual psyche. Psyches exhibiting a very dominant imaginative power, or emotional power, or intellectual power (for example), tend to fall into distinctly different character types. Though each psyche differs in terms of the distribution of the influence of the powers, these tend to fall into standard configurations (or "presets"), which provide a basis for character type.

(b) Subjective/Intuitive view

As the foregoing section shows, the faculties may be examined analytically. We can watch the faculties in action, on their own as well as in their interactions. We can judge their relative weight and influence on any given state of mind, particularly the *status animus*. But the *status animus,* from the understanding's point of view, is merely a concept. It is a concept of a whole with interdependent parts. Represented as a *status* or state, the dynamic of the faculties is falsified, robbed of its motion and ever-changing nature. A state is a snapshot that freezes motion, capturing only a point in time. Thus it misrepresents its subject, but at least presents the idea of the relative influence of each mental power upon the whole of the psyche.

But we are also intuitively aware of the dynamic of mental life. Intuitively the powers do not operate independently of each other, but rather each is inextricably woven into every experience. There is no such thing as pure feeling, emotion, imagining, willing or thinking; each requires the others to function. In each inner act, one mental power may give the primary impetus, and the influence of the other powers may vary greatly, but is not absent. For example, in an deeply emotional state like despair, the will may become virtually disabled. In a deeply imaginative state, the functions of the intellect—understanding, logic, reasoning—may be virtually cancelled. Indeed that may be the artist's intention. But the painting could never have been drafted without the involvement of the intellect, however slight.

Through direct introspection, we can feel an imbalance among the powers; and we can equally feel the psyche return to a default or "normal" inner state, to a "balance of powers" so to speak. In the constant flow of sensations, images, feelings, and thoughts, rising, interacting, and falling away, we witness the wellspring of ever-resurgent life. Life itself plays out on the mind's eye no less fabulously than upon the outer eye. We call this second approach, which acknowledges the parts, but experiences the dynamic of faculties as a whole, "intuitive".

By the intuitive approach, we directly sense the "free play" of the various mental powers as they jockey for influence in our psyche. We can sense the ascendance of one faculty over the others for temporary control of the psyche. Under varying circumstances—for example in response to changes in the immediate environment, or in states of mental or emotional excitement, the relative weight or influence of each faculty varies. It may be that the understanding is fully engaged and dominant in the psyche at one moment, when an abrupt emotional challenge—perhaps an argument with a loved one—changes that balance drastically. Emotion flares, imagination works overtime, understanding retreats—the dynamic of the inner powers has decidedly shifted.

Powerful sensations and warm emotions eventually cool; the balance between the inner powers, once upset, eventually returns to "normal", i.e., the psyche's default state. Notwithstanding the sometimes wild dynamic of the faculties, there is always a return to the *status animus,* in which the powers revert to their predetermined relationships, i.e., their proportion of influence. A hidden balance or law or mechanism—a kind of *harmonia praestabilita*—governs these relationships.

The immediate experience or intuition of the *status animus* is *not* esoteric. In fact there is nothing more familiar than one's own default state of mind. Every person with a modicum of self-awareness can identify their "default" mental state. And we are very familiar with our partners' or loved ones' typical state of mind, their "normal" mood. Moods are rarely unique states of mind, but rather familiar. The reason is that moods consist of standard faculty configurations, and these configurations, or presets, occur again and again.

The intuition of the harmony of the inner powers is *not* abstract, but rather personal; it is one's *own* psyche. Their harmony produces a sense of proportion, inner calm and well-being which is pleasurable. Within it, for example, the ever-demanding will, or the greedy intellect settle at length into a more ancient harmony, with a more egalitarian distribution of the mental powers. (For sense perception, emotion, and imagination were more powerful in early man, as Vico first observed.) Moreover there is pleasure in the sheer spectacle of the interaction of natural forces. In the intuition of inner life we witness nature itself unfolding in real time. The intuition of the mental powers as forces of nature is the intuition of necessity.

E. The Meaning of Character

What is the meaning of character for self-knowledge and action? In Greek tragedy the hero is not an individual but a character with a fixed set of traits, for example arrogant or prideful or impetuous or deceitful. This was reinforced by the character's mask, which allowed multiple actors in any given performance to play a single character. This is also seen in the chorus, which consisted of multiple actors wearing the same mask, collectively representing a single character. Of course an actor might endow the character with realistic traits through voice and body movement. But his actions were due not to his individuality, which might show spontaneity or freedom, but by his type, which is determined through and through. For it is through the character type, not individual traits, that the audience participates in the universal. The universal is the inscrutable domain of the gods, and of fate. In character, the individual is subsumed by the universal.

There are three main ways a character may meet their fate: (a) with resistance (the usual way); (b) with resignation; or (c) with love. Character meets fate either (a) negatively, (b) neutrally, or (c) positively. Like a tragic hero we may resist our fate, even as necessity rises against us. Or, we may be resigned to it. But there is a third way: we may embrace it. This embrace has a name: *amor fati,* love of fate.[8]

F. The Meaning of Necessity

Character reveals to the goal-seeker the meaning of necessity. When failure finally strikes, the individual seeker, falling back on the foundation of his nature, grasps what is necessary, what he *must* do. In character the seeker discovers the "hard bottom" of his nature. Seen through character, "necessity" provides a *positive moral* significance. By fully grasping necessity, the remainder—the sphere of freedom and choice—is more readily seen. The seeker must decide whether he will commit to his fate—not merely yield and give way to it, but choose it. *Amor fati* is love of necessity. By loving his fate, the seeker chooses to act—as he must—according to his character.

G. *Amor Fati*

We flog ourselves for thinking we might have acted differently in the past. We may feel sharp pangs of remorse. But

---

8 Friedrich Nietzsche, *The Gay Science,* trans. Walter Kaufman, trans. (New York: Vintage Books, 1974.) Para. 276.

in fact what happened *had* to happen—exactly when and how it did. We were *not* free at that moment to act otherwise. And yet, we still take responsibility for events—not because we are the actual cause of them, but because in doing so, we assert our freedom.

Though there is no free will, and we know it, we nevertheless act as if there is—as we must. For without the notion of freedom, how could we understand individual responsibility? To assume wholesale responsibility for myriad events one could not have caused is irrational, but also a demonstration of freedom. For upon the presumption of freedom and the assertion of individual agency rests the possibility of morality.

Accepting the determinism of the will directly poses the question of our individual fate. We cannot control fate, but we can control—we can freely choose—our attitude toward it. *Resistance* of fate is the most common attitude, but it is by definition a lost battle. Resignation accepts fate at least; but it is passive and undermines the will and all our reasons for action. To move beyond the mere denial or the mere suffering of our fate, we must call it our own and embrace it. By identifying with necessity, we can then choose it. By affirming every determining condition, we close the open circuit separating subject and object, mind and matter. This is the meaning of amor *fati*, love of fate.

Amor fati goes beyond passive acceptance of necessity—it seeks to embrace it. It rushes headlong, searching for its own end. Since the formerly opposed substances of subject and object are now merged, now joined in fate, this special love—*amor fati*—offers the possibility of a reconciliation with nature. Paradoxically, it is not by our freedom but by our determinism that we achieve human nature's highest expression.

A complete understanding of one's character can only be gained through the awareness of how necessity operates on it, and whether to resist or embrace it. In the fully self-aware character, choice is a paradox: we must understand how external necessity operates upon us—then choose this necessity *as our own*. We both *deliberately* choose our fate and *must* choose our fate. This is the paradox of *amor fati.*

Endnotes

1. Miloš Janáček, *Reach for Greatness.* New York: Harper Torchbooks, 2013. Chapter 8, "What Is Character?" (See Appendix B in this book for complete extract.)
2. Arthur Schopenhauer (Konstantin Kolenda, tr.), *Essay on the Freedom of the Will.* Mineola, NY: Dover Publications, 2005. Page 19.
3. Miloš Janáček (Miloš Janáček, tr.), *The Phenomenon of Choice* (Chapter 3, "The Paradox of Goals"). Prague: Pragma, 2007.) Page 72ff. (See Appendix A in this book for complete extract.)
4. Ibid.
5. Werner Herzog (writer, director), *Aguirre, the Wrath of God.* (Berlin: Werner Herzog Filmproduktion Hessischer Rundfunk, 1972.).
6. Schopenhauer.
7. Ibid, p. 17.
8. Ibid, p. 22ff.
9. Dan Sullivan, "How to be a Successful Entrepreneur." (Strategic Coach: The Multiplier Mindset Blog) http://blog.strategiccoach.com/how-to-be-a-successful-entrepreneur. Accessed Nov. 18, 2017.
10. Søren Kierkegaard (Alexander Dru., tr.), *The Present Age.* (New York: Harper & Row, 1962.) Page 51ff.
11. Paul Tillich, *The Courage to Be.* (New Haven: Yale University Press, 1952.) Pages 36-39.
12. Schopenhauer (2005). Page 16.

13. J. Priestley, *Doctrine of Philosophical Necessity.* (Birmingham: 1782). Pages 26, 37, 43, 66, 84, 90, 287. Quotation from Schopenhauer (2005). Pages 80-81.
14. Priestley.
15. Immanuel Kant (Werner Pluhar, tr.), *Critique of Judgment.* (Indianapolis: Hackett, 1987.) Page 61.
16. Rainer Maria Rilke (Stephen Mitchell, tr.), "Archaic Torso of Apollo". In *Ahead of All Parting: Selected Poetry and Prose of Rainer Maria Rilke.* (New York: Modern Library, 1995.)
17. Friedrich Nietzsche (Shaun Whiteside, tr.), *The Birth of Tragedy.* (London: Penguin, 1992.) Pages 16, 17.
18. Søren Kierkegaard (Douglas V. Steere, tr.), *Purity of Heart Is to Will One Thing.* (New York: Harper & Row, 1948, 1956.) Page 107ff.
19. Ibid.
20. Anonymous, "Neuro-linguistic Programming." In Wikipedia: The Free Encyclopedia. (San Francisco: Wikimedia Foundation, Inc.) https://en.wikipedia.org/wiki/Neuro-linguistic_programming. Accessed April 21, 2016. As stated in subsection "Therapeutic Applications": Clinical psychologist Stephen Briers questions the value of the NLP maxim—a presupposition in NLP jargon—"there is no failure, only feedback." Briers argues that the denial of the existence of failure diminishes its instructive value. He offers Walt Disney, Isaac Newton and J.K. Rowling as three examples of unambiguously acknowledged personal failure that served as an impetus to great success. According to Briers, it was "the crash-and-burn type of failure, not the sanitized NLP Failure Lite, i.e. the failure-that-isn't-really-failure sort of failure" that propelled these individuals to success. Briers contends that adherence to the maxim leads to self-deprecation. According to Briers, personal

endeavor is a product of invested values and aspirations and the dismissal of personally significant failure as mere feedback effectively denigrates what one values. Briers writes, "Sometimes we need to accept and mourn the death of our dreams, not just casually dismiss them as inconsequential. NLP's reframe casts us into the role of a widower avoiding the pain of grief by leap-frogging into a rebound relationship with a younger woman, never pausing to say a proper goodbye to his dead wife." Briers also contends that the NLP maxim is narcissistic, self-centered and divorced from notions of moral responsibility.

21. Virginia Woolf, Mrs. Dalloway. (London: Hogarth, 1925.) Page 15ff.
22. Ibid.
23. Virgil, *Aenead*. VI.126-129.) The Aeneid: Interlinear Translation, Frederick Holland Dewey, tr. Wildside Press, 1917

    ...easy is the descent to Avernus;
    Night and day the door of black Pluto lies open;
    But to retrace thy step and escape to the upper air,
    that is truly work and toil.

24. Tillich. Page 40.
25. Tillich. Page 34.
26. John "Fire" Lame Deer, as quoted in Elise K. Kirk, American Opera. (Champaign, IL: University of Illinois Press, 2001.) Page 145.
27. William Blake, "Auguries of Innocence". In David V. Erdman (ed.), *The Complete Poetry & Prose of William Blake.* (New York: Random House, 1988.) Page 491.